THE DOCTOR IS OUT

On my way down the hallway, I noticed that the double doors guarding Baxter's neighbor's office stood open. A muffled gurgling noise halted my charge for the stairs. Should I tell Baxter? I knew it would involve bursting in on another patient's time and reporting what would most likely turn out to be a figment of my presently overworked imagination.

I continued past the open doors. Something in the room then gurgled again, slower this time. I turned back and peered into the open doctor's office. The doctor lay sprawled on his back beside the desk with a hole punched in his neck. The wound gurgled as blood seeped into the carpet.

I screamed.

"So intelligent and engaging, even readers who don't know a driver from a nine-iron will love it."

—Abigail Padgett

Six Strokes Under

Roberta Isleib

Hit em straynt!
Roberta Isleib

BERKLEY PRIME CRIME, NEW YORK

For John,
who caddies for all my dreams

My warmest thanks go to:

LPGA staff Kathy Lawrence and Neal Reid, the staff and members of the Plantation Golf and Country Club, especially John Talbott; and Bunker and Divot, for making my own trip to Q-school a breeze.

The players and their mothers, including Jessica Popiel, Diane Irvin, and especially Kim O'Connor, for sharing stories of their real Q-school experience.

John, Molly, Andrew, and all of my extended family.

Fellow writers and editors Chris Falcone, Dale Peterson, Angelo Pompano, Dale Eddy, Katharine Weber, Sue Repko, Maureen Robb, Susan Cerulean, John Brady, and Joy Johannessen.

Friends and friendly readers Yvonne Sparling, Diane Burbank, Jane and Jack Novick, Lesley Siegel, Debbie Griswold, Susan Gilfillan, Carol Ballentine, Paula Fischer, Tim Boyd, Curt Fisher, Howard Blue, Jono Miller, and Don Gliha.

My friends at Business and Legal Reports, for making a forest's worth of draft copies.

RJ Julia's Bookstore and the First Congregational Church in Madison, for providing places to meet and talk about writing.

Paige Wheeler, for persisting. The IWWG and Sheree Bykovsky, for helping me find her. Cindy Hwang for believing in the project.

All my pals at the MCC, for tolerating an endless parade of mediocre shots and sub-par language. *Caveat ludens.*

Glossary

Approach Shot: a golf shot used to reach the green, generally demanding accuracy, rather than distance

Back nine: second half of the eighteen-hole golf course; usually holes ten through eighteen

Birdie: a score of one stroke fewer than par for the hole

Bogey: a score of one stroke over par for the hole; double bogey is two over par; triple bogey is three over

Bunker: a depression containing sand; also called a sand trap or simply a trap

Caddie: person designated or hired to carry the golfer's bag and advise him/her on golf course strategy

Card: status that allows the golfer to compete on the PGA or LPGA Tour

Chip: a short, lofted golf shot used to reach the green from a relatively close position

Chunk: to strike the ground inadvertently before hitting the ball; similar to chili-dipping, dubbing, and hitting it fat

Collar: the fringe of grass surrounding the perimeter of the green

Cup: the plastic cylinder lining the inside of the hole; the hole itself

Cut: the point halfway through a tournament at which the number of competitors is reduced based on their cumulative scores

Divot: a gouge in the turf resulting from a golf shot; also, the chunk of turf that was gouged out

Leaderboard: display board on which top players in a tournament are listed

Lie: the position of the ball on the course

Out of bounds: a ball hit outside of the legal boundary of the golf course which results in a two-stroke penalty for the golfer; also called OB

Par: the number of strokes set as the standard for a hole, or for an entire course

Pin: the flagstick

Pitch: a short, lofted shot most often taken with a wedge

Putt: a stroke using a putter on the green intended to advance the ball towards the hole

Qualifying school (Q-school): a series of rounds of golf played in the fall which produces a small number of top players who will be eligible to play on the LPGA Tour that year

Rainmaker: an unusually high shot

Range: a practice area

Round: eighteen holes of golf

Rough: the area of the golf course along the sides of the fairway that is not closely mown; also, the grass in the rough

Shank: a faulty golf shot hit off the shank or hosel of the club that generally travels sharply right

Skull: a short swing that hits the top half of the ball and results in a line-drive trajectory

Slice: a golf shot which starts out straight and curves to the right (for right-handers)

Tee: the area of the golf hole designated as the starting point, delineated by tee markers, behind which the golfer must set up

Chapter 1

The *South Carolina Sun News* lay on the kitchen table, folded open to the want ads. Mom had gone through the listings with a yellow highlighter. *Pastry chef, responsible for breakfast, desserts, and banquet production.* Me in a chef's toque? I'd never scrambled an egg without her one-on-one supervision. *Job coach for the disabled, experience in special ed and bilingual (Spanish) preferred.* I knew *hola* and *gracias. Telemarketing, business-to-business, hard selling required.* I couldn't sell Girl Scout cookies to my own grandparents. *Restaurant counter help, intelligent and upbeat.* Intelligent? Sometimes. Upbeat? Not so you could count on it.

Besides the astonishing lack of fit between me and her selections, Mom had overlooked the fact that I was flying to Sarasota in three days for the LPGA qualifying school, otherwise known as Q-school, a boot camp for wannabe professional golfers. The lesson plan, four days of mental and physical torment, determined who'd get a shot at be-

me this crap about finding yourself, sister. Trust me when I tell you my authentic self does not involve serving enough cholesterol every morning to choke the arteries of every golfer in the state. Though that isn't a bad idea."

"You've got the poor bastard nailed." Laura laughed. "I take it head breakfast cook is not his life's dream."

"He doesn't know how to dream. He hit a new low yesterday when he brought home an application from Hooters, home of fast food served by big boobs."

"Hey, don't knock waitressing. Your mom does it. I did it all through college. And Hooters's chicken wings rule."

"Have you seen what they make those girls wear? Skin-tight orange nylon shorts that can't begin to cover their cheeks. I bet you don't even fill out an application to work there, just write down your name and bra size in big block letters. Cassandra Burdette, thirty-six C."

"In your dreams, girl," Laura said through snorts of laughter. "Come to think of it, you probably don't have the right equipment for that position."

More laughter. Best friend or not, she was starting to seriously wear me out.

"Any word from Jack?" she asked.

"Nothing new. He's in Japan this week, so the time zones and the long-distance rates are killing us." I'd met Jack just before I left my caddie job on the PGA Tour. His rocky performance as a rookie golfer meant he was banished to the Asian Tour until his game picked up. Just thinking about him gave me a little physical jolt, a frisson, I think the Victorian ladies would have called it. Even though he split before our flirtation had time to catch fire, I had two dreams on the horizon now: the LPGA Tour and Jack Wolfe.

"Gotta run," I said. "I'm going over to the club to hit balls. I'll pick you up in Florida Monday afternoon. Call

bounced with each step as he trotted to the clubhouse ahead of me.

"You taking a little money on the side hawking Lucky Charms?" my older brother, Charlie, asked Dad the first time he saw the new uniforms.

"It may look like schlock to you," Dad said, "but it's our edge over the competition."

"Just don't let the NAACP play the tenth hole," Charlie said. That was my favorite spot on the course, where a black guy in a chef's hat and apron served chicken gumbo from a pot hanging over a wood fire next to the tee.

"We may not have the length or challenge of some of the other courses," Dad told Charlie, "but where else does Scarlett O'Hara meet Jack Nicklaus?"

Inside the pro shop, I walked past the black-and-white photograph of the club taken in 1965. Every person on staff posed on the front lawn, along with every piece of course maintenance equipment, including a 1963 Buick station wagon, a '62 Pontiac, and seven hand lawnmowers. The ladies wore Jackie Kennedy pillbox hats on their flip hairdos. My very young father had just been hired. He wore a Butch wax special and a huge grin.

Odell Washington rubbed my back while I waited for the assistant pro to bring me a bucket of golf balls. I leaned into his kneading fingers.

"Feeling okay today, sweetheart?" he asked.

Odell had worked alongside Dad for eighteen of Dad's twenty years. Being black and over fifty, he hadn't been at all surprised to be passed over for promotion when the head pro job came open. Then he ended up with the spot after all when the Florida hot shot absconded with the pro shop till at the end of his first season. Eight months ago, I'd come limping home from caddying on the PGA Tour with a serious case of post-traumatic stress syndrome, related to some rookie's errant drive landing between my

mon." He pulled me down the row of golfers until we stood behind her.

"Kaitlin Rupert, Cassie Burdette." I extended my hand. She laid hers limply in mine.

"Cassie's just come off a stint caddying on the PGA Tour. She looped for Mike Callahan through Q-school and his rookie year," Odell said.

"Interesting," said Kaitlin, turning back to her bag. Not to her, I guess.

"Kaitlin's headed to Q-school next week, too. Maybe you could give her some tips on what she can expect," Odell said to me.

"I've already hired Butch Harmon for a consultation. That's Tiger's coach," Kaitlin said. "So I'm all set. Unless you think you have some tips he won't have thought of." She laughed, picked up a short iron, and resumed hitting pitch shots.

What a bitch.

Odell grabbed the back of my T-shirt and tugged me a couple of stations away. "I know she seems difficult, but she needs someone right now." His voice dropped to a conspiratorial whisper. "She's got family problems that could really get in her way."

Line up and join the damn club.

"You know her father," said Odell. "Peter Rupert. He was the football coach at the high school."

Everyone in Myrtle Beach knew Rupert. He'd been my brother Charlie's idol for the better part of his teenage years, much to Dad's chagrin.

"She needs a shoulder right now," said Odell, "or everything she's worked for will go down the toilet."

That sounded familiar, too. I poked at a range ball with the toe of my wedge.

"With your experience taking Mike through Q-school, you'd be a major asset."

"It's an entirely different experience when you're the one standing over those putts in this kind of competition. Until you've been through it over and over, six feet might as well be sixty yards."

I shrugged. She was probably right, but the snotty attitude galled me.

"You must have money to burn," she said. "Or maybe you're just out of your mind."

"Neither one," I said. "Just optimistic."

Just another optimistic asshole, I wished I'd had the nerve to say.

I walked back to my bag, hoping I looked confident, not mushy-kneed and queasy, the way I felt inside. I couldn't let myself dwell on the misgivings Kaitlin had stirred up. Or my own burning question, exactly the one she'd raised. Where the hell did I get off thinking I was going to make it on the LPGA Tour with no experience but a few college competitions and a year caddying?

The situation called for action. The kind of action I could get for a few bucks sitting at the bar of the Chili Dip Inn.

Myrtle Beach High School football coach Peter Rupert has been arrested and charged with sexual abuse by his daughter, Kaitlin Rupert. Max Harding, attorney for the defendant, refused to comment on the specific allegations made by Ms. Rupert. Said Harding, "I can only state that recovered memories of abuse have been one of the most controversial concepts in the field of psychology in the past decade. There have been many instances of over-zealous psychotherapists implanting false memories in their patients. I cannot say whether this has occurred with Ms. Rupert, but I will state that my client has never abused her, sexually or otherwise." Harding also refused comment on alleged quotes from a member of his staff that Ms. Rupert was "participating in a modern-day witch-hunt" and "falling victim to the false memory syndrome epidemic."

Mom had used the yellow highlighter every time Max Harding's name appeared in the article. Shit.

A chorus of Mom's cuckoo clocks reminded me that I had promised Odell I'd open the shop at 6:30 A.M. Almost late already, I dropped the paper and hurried off to shower and dress.

While the hot shower water beat the knots in my back loose, I thought about Max Harding. I hoped I wouldn't run into him while he was in town. If I did run into him, I hoped he'd developed a receding hairline and a belly that lopped over the waist of his Sansabelt slacks. If he wasn't bald and fat, I hoped he would notice that I weighed the same as I did in high school, only now it was 110 pounds of toned muscle.

Then I wondered about Coach Rupert. Mom used to

"I don't have time to fool around. Coach says football has to come first if we want the championship that badly." And that came after Dad asked him if he wanted to play handball, or hit a bucket of range balls, or join him in just about any activity you could name.

I think Dad recognized by then that his life's work consisted of giving lessons to tourists who weren't going to listen to him anyway, and that nothing would ever change as long as he stayed in South Carolina. Hearing Coach lifted up as the archangel of wisdom for teenage boys was finally more than he could stand.

"Go eat your fucking dinner at his house, then!" he exploded one night. "Maybe he'll pay your goddamned college tuition, too."

Charlie tossed his napkin on the table and pushed in his chair. "He's two times the man you'll ever be," he said as he left.

I offered to go beat balls at the range with Dad, but he turned me down. I wanted to kill Charlie. Mom just cried.

I turned off the water and toweled off roughly, wishing I could rub out those old memories. I searched through my closet and found a pair of chinos with a faint press line, and a pink golf shirt. A white-and-tan-striped vest covered the coffee stain on the shirt. Then I clipped on a pair of gold earrings in the shape of golf balls and looked in the mirror. Professional, but just feminine enough, I hoped. I knew nothing in my wardrobe was going to raise me into Kaitlin's league. Charlie would have said I sold myself short. Not hard to do when the entire advertising world tells you you're dirt unless you're tall and blond, two attributes which did not apply to me.

I arrived at the club at 7:15, damp-haired and remorseful. Odell had already opened up the register.

"Never mind helping here," said Odell. "You need to get out to the range and get to work."

"Only the headline," I lied. "I'm sorry for your troubles."

"Full of pompous quotes from the famous defense attorney Max Harding," she said. "I heard you and he were an item."

"That was over ten years ago," I said, squirming. "I wouldn't know him now if I tripped over him."

"He's a horse's ass," she said. "Even if my father had a decent case, which he doesn't, Attorney Harding would screw it up."

I shrugged. Max was real smart back when I knew him, but I sure wasn't going out on any limb defending him now, particularly not to her. I broke eye contact with her and peered into her golf bag. "Damn, that's some pretty fancy gear you have."

Kaitlin pulled her bag back out of my line of vision. "Deikon is sponsoring me this year. I'm trying some new stuff out for them, top of the line. Not out in the market yet."

"Like that golf ball Tiger was using," I said, laughing. "Now there was a public relations nightmare. All the hackers in America rushing in to buy a ball that only existed in Tiger's bag. Hey, those new clubs don't have the trampoline-effect faces, do they? You'd hate to be disqualified before you even got going."

The average golfer was always looking for the technical advantage that would increase the length of his drives—preferably something that wouldn't involve practice. Just lately, the United States Golf Association had decided that the newest technology, allowing golf balls to spring off the club face like a trampoline, was taking the whole trend too far.

"The clubs I use conform completely with every specification in the book," Kaitlin said, extracting a copy of

Chapter 3

When I got home that afternoon, I called my friend Joe Lancaster. Joe was a psychologist who'd given up his practice with ordinary people to work with athletically talented, but equally nutty, professional golfers. He told me their problems might be different—like "my three-foot putts won't drop" instead of "my husband and I aren't communicating"—but the pain was all the same.

I described the snit Kaitlin had pitched at the range. "I don't get it," I said. "How can an adult behave that way in public with her own mother? She's not thirteen, for God's sake."

"I haven't met her, so it's not fair to guess," Joe said.

"When has that ever held you back?" I asked. "Go ahead. Start talking."

He laughed. "If you insist . . . sounds like borderline features."

"And in plain English that means . . ."

antiquated equipment. Then there was the scene with her mother. Still, I feel kind of sorry for her. And Odell thinks I could help."

"You want my free advice?" said Joe. "Stick to golf. Forget about the peer counseling. Patients who have this kind of history and are willing to get involved in that kind of controversy scream personality disorder. You could sink into a bog you'd never climb back out of."

Frankly, for a psychologist who made his living helping people, even people as difficult as Kaitlin, I thought his assessment was a little mean-spirited.

"I bet you're thinking I should be more compassionate," said Joe. "What's the girl like?"

"She's a looker," I said. "Blond hair, big boobs, the whole nine yards. You'd be drooling all over yourself." My turn to be mean-spirited.

"Give me a little credit here," he said.

"Credit for what? Have you forgotten Georgia so soon?" I hadn't forgotten Georgia—a blowsy, oversexed, lavishly perfumed, bleached-blond bombshell that he'd taken up with last summer to ease the transition away from his failing marriage. A little too much human frailty for a shrink to display, in my humble opinion. Especially since we'd had electricity crackling between us from the moment we met. Until Georgia showed up and blew the fuse in that circuit. Now, as far as I was concerned, Joe and me—we were just plain pals.

Joe interrupted my thoughts with a groan. "Okay, after I wiped the drool off my chin, what else would I notice about her?"

"Focus," I said. "She had the entire male population of the driving range sporting woodies and all she saw was her own swing path."

"Sporting woodies?"

I knew if I got there late, we'd waste half the hour talking about the deep psychological ramifications of my tardiness, but on the other hand, I hated to get there too early and end up having to cool my heels with the losers waiting for his officemate, Dr. Bencher. Bencher looked normal enough—standard-issue close-cropped goatee, white button-down shirt with sleeves rolled up, sometimes a vest, sometimes a tie. All designed, I imagined, to give that professional yet rumpled and warm effect conducive to the spilling of guts.

But unlike Baxter and his merry band of high-functioning neurotics, Bencher seemed to specialize in the genuine crazies. God knows, maybe they thought I was wacko, too. But at least I didn't sit in the waiting area clanking through the bag of filthy cans I'd collected from the Dumpster outside the back door. Or wear a baseball cap with an Insane Clown Posse logo and rows of carpet tacks glued around the brim, pointy ends out.

I released the latch on the bucket seat of my Volvo and leaned back with my eyes closed to meditate to the sweet sounds of Patsy Cline. I had five minutes to fantasize about a steamy reunion with Jack Wolfe.

A siren interrupted Patsy's lament. Then I heard shouts in the parking lot outside Dr. Baxter's building. I got out of the car to investigate. Two men and a woman in business suits marched in front of the door waving placards and yelling. It wasn't the first time I'd had to wend my way through a receiving line of protesters—my shrink's suitemate seemed to gravitate to controversy.

"It's bad enough coming here at all," I'd told Dr. Baxter last time this happened. "But running a gauntlet of crackpots to get here . . ." I could only shake my head.

The businesspeople carried signs that read, "Manufactured Memories: Shattered Lives," "Charlatan Shrinks Stroll Down Pseudo-Memory Lane," and "Stick to Anal-

touching your tongue to a rotten tooth." He leaned back in his chair and stroked his beard, a pose I thought he must have learned in shrink school. Something they pull out when they're moving in for the kill but don't want to alarm the prey. "You have other choices," he said. "How does it really feel to be going to qualifying school?"

"Okay," I said. "Fine."

He sighed. "Your mother stays stuck in her old feelings. You sometimes don't let yourself know what yours are."

"What does that mean?" I said. "I know what I feel. I just don't see the point of wallowing around in the past. You want me to break down and blubber about how scared I am. How's that going to help me?"

"You keep a distance from your feelings," said Dr. Baxter. "You're like a caddie to your own life—reading the wind, checking how the ball lies, studying the yardage book. You wait for someone else to hit the shot, rather than get involved."

I rolled my eyes. Like he had a clue about being a caddie. It was just as hard as playing golf, maybe harder. You had to carry the emotional weight of someone else's performance without having even a shred of real control over how the thing turned out. Let him spend one afternoon lugging Mike Callahan's bag around a golf course, trying to keep him from blowing sky high. Then he could tell me I wasn't involved.

"Q-school sounds like good news," said Dr. Baxter, interrupting my internal rampage. "You're putting yourself back in your life, not standing by watching on the sidelines."

I didn't say anything. I wasn't trying to be difficult or rude. But I still wasn't comfortable with this therapy thing, this constant stream of personal feedback, often way more than I wanted to hear, from someone I really hardly knew. And most annoying of all, he was usually

Chapter 4

On my way down the exit hallway, I noticed that the double doors guarding Baxter's neighbor's office stood cracked open several inches. This was not up to Dr. Bencher's usual standard of security. Not that I blamed him for being careful. I, too, would have preferred to keep two steel-reinforced doors and a peephole between me and the sea of human flotsam that bobbed about in the safe harbor of his waiting room.

A muffled gurgling noise halted my beeline charge for the stairs. I heard the noise again—not so much gurgling this time as rasping, like someone who seriously could not breathe. I decided to go back and tell Baxter—let him check on Bencher.

But when I reached the waiting area, Baxter's door had been shut, and the heavy-set, miserable-looking woman who often followed my session no longer sat in the chair by the window. Damn. Now alerting Baxter to the weird noise would involve bursting into her reserved hour and

I screamed. I leaped up and backed into the corridor yelling for help. Then I stepped back over Bencher's body and dialed 911. The police, who must have continued hassling the protesters during the length of my session, arrived quickly. Dr. Baxter was next, his fat, unhappy patient trailing behind him. The first officer on the scene interviewed me briefly, then grabbed Bencher's footstool, dragged it to a corner of the room, and pointed.

"Sit," said the officer, whose name tag identified him as Sergeant Dixon. "Don't touch anything."

I watched him speak with Baxter and his patient in the hallway. Then he returned to help cordon off the crime scene, while paramedics attended to the psychiatrist. As I sat, facing away from the doctor's body, my nostrils filled with a strong metallic odor. I knew it was his blood.

I remembered a technique Joe taught me for blocking out distracting or unpleasant thoughts on the golf course. "If your mind is busy cataloging horizontal and vertical lines in your environment," he said, "it pushes the panic and negativity right out. Don't analyze the lines, just notice them." Bookshelves: vertical. Countertop: horizontal. Directory of South Carolina Psychiatric Services: horizontal. Pole lamp: vertical.

As I worked my way across the room, I noticed the disarray in the adjoining filing cubby. Manila folders were tossed in heaps on the floor and the drawers of the cabinets had been left dangling open. A small glass coffeepot lay shattered on the floor, its contents soaking into the folders. Without thinking, I walked over and began to blot the liquid up off the binders with a roll of paper towels I found on the counter.

"I said don't touch anything!" shouted Sergeant Dixon. I sat again. Now my teeth rattled—I felt cold and sick, any illusion of calm shattered. The paramedics covered the doctor's wound, fastened an oxygen mask around his

"No." I doubted he wanted to hear my unfounded opinions about the parade of weirdos I'd seen march through the waiting room each week. Or maybe he would, but then I'd rate a do-not-pass-go ride to the loony bin.

"You're free to leave now," said the detective. "But we'll need you to stay in the area over the next week in case we have further questions."

"That's not possible," I said, beginning to cry. "I'm leaving for qualifying school the day after tomorrow."

"It's a golf tournament," said Dr. Baxter, moving a few steps closer to where we stood. "She'll be back by next weekend. Maybe you could give the officers your cell phone number so they can call if you're needed?"

Finally, with Dr. Baxter's reassuring intervention, the police allowed me to go.

I headed directly to Chili-Dippers. Paul, the bartender, laid a napkin featuring kidney beans square-dancing with hot peppers on the bar in front of me, then set a draft Budweiser in a frosted mug on the napkin. All this before my butt had even settled onto the barstool. The perks of being promoted to a regular.

"I'll take a shot of tequila, too," I said. "Long, long day."

Just the sameness of the bar felt comforting. On the far wall hung pictures of every football team that ever came out of Myrtle Beach High. From 1970 on, Coach Rupert was in all of them, exhibiting a toothy grin you never saw on the ball field. The golf team portraits were posted high above the football teams. My father stood in the back row in the pictures from the sixties and seventies. Each year, his smile looked a little more strained, until he finally disappeared altogether—burned out on coaching. In the photos from my junior and senior years, I was the only

to go back week after next, because now we'd gotten tangled up in a whole new way.

As I sipped my Bud, fragments of a conversation occurring down the bar came into focus.

"How was he killed?"

"Bullet right between the eyes," said a man at the bar, flicking a finger of ash from his cigarette onto the floor.

"Did you hear this, Cassie?" Paul called over to me. "The headshrinker involved in the Rupert sex abuse case was found murdered this afternoon. Who do they like for the shooting?" Paul asked his informant.

The smoker shrugged. "Too early to say, I guess."

"He was shot in the neck, not between the eyes," I said, sliding my beer down the bar to join the conversation. "Are they sure he's dead?"

The smoker nodded.

"Hot off the press," said Paul, his eyebrows raised at me. "What was his name?"

"Dr. Bencher. Gregory Bencher."

"How come you got the news flash on where he was shot?"

"He has an office on Seaview," I said. "I rode by there today and stopped when I saw all the commotion." No way was I going to admit that I'd seen the hubbub up close and personal because I was leaving my own shrink appointment.

"I know that guy," said Paul. "He has a way of mixing it up with clients that put him in the limelight. Hasn't he been testifying for the Harrington custody case?"

"Saw him on the five o'clock news just last week," said the smoker. "Both the parents sounded like they're fresh out of the asylum. I feel sorry for the kid, either way the thing turns out."

"This time, Bencher's made the spotlight for sure." Paul's tongue made a clucking sound as he wiped down

bald nor fat. Hunched down behind the menu, I listened to him order a beer and join the banter of the men lining the bar.

"What can you tell us about Bencher?" Paul asked. "Does this put a hole in your case, prime witness with a hole in his head and all?"

Max laughed, a deep baritone, bordering on bass, that I remembered just as clearly as if I'd told him a joke yesterday. "You know I can't tell you anything, Pauly. But we have lots of other witnesses. This has to hurt their case more than ours."

Sharlene, the waitress, approached me from behind and tapped my shoulder. "Do y'all want to order something, darlin'? We have two specials tonight. Open-faced roast beef on toast with mashed potatoes and gravy or hash and poached." In spite of the name and the cocktail napkins, the food at Chili-Dippers was about as far from Mexican as you could stretch.

"I haven't decided," I whispered from behind the menu.

"I can't hear you, darlin'," she said, pushing the menu away from my face.

"The roast beef," I said, just wanting her to go away.

"Maxie, have you met Cassie Burdette? She's a caddie on the PGA Tour."

"Was a caddie," I said, lowering my shield in defeat. Max just stared.

I gestured to the bartender to bring me another round. "Nice to see you," I said to Max. As if we'd just exchanged pleasantries last week. As if it hadn't been ten years since he'd sweet-talked me into sleeping with him on the beach after the prom, with the help of a bottle of Boone's Farm Apple Wine and the pulsing rhythm of the Atlantic Ocean. Ten years since he'd barely spoken to me the following day or any of the days following that one.

He glanced at his watch. Then a wave of red washed up his neck, flooded across his jawline, and bled into his cheeks. "Sorry. I'm meeting Brenda for dinner. I'm already late." He gathered his trench coat from the barstool and reached for his wallet. "Let me get this young lady's bill, too."

"Not in this lifetime," I said, in a voice so hard even the drunk three stools down from me looked up in surprise. Brenda was the cheerleader who'd replaced me a couple of months after Max shut me out. I'd heard from Mom she'd married Max five or so years ago—promoted to cheerleader for life. Let him buy her drinks. I would get blasted on my own tab, thank you very much.

I watched Max leave the bar. "Once an asshole, always an asshole," said a stocky man who slid into an open seat beside me. "Gary Rupert. You remember me, don't you? Katie's my baby sister. And don't worry, Brenda's still got the biggest ass Myrtle Beach High School ever saw. In more ways than one." He laughed loudly and pulled his stool closer to mine.

Jesus. It was beginning to feel like the set from *Cheers* in this bar tonight—everyone I'd ever known was making a cameo appearance. I had no trouble remembering Gary. He'd asked me out several times after Max dumped me. With my sixteen-year-old heart broken, I wouldn't have gone out on a date even if my fantasy heartthrob Robert Redford had called. And Gary was no teenaged Robert Redford. Where Kaitlin had inherited the long-limbed, aristocratic features of her mother and the athleticism of her father, Gary had gotten the reverse—his mom's clumsiness and Coach's looks, only more squat and lumpy, and minus his father's charm. Maybe it was the beer and the tequila shooter I'd just swallowed, but it seemed like he'd improved on all those fronts over the intervening years.

Chapter 5

◁
⟲ **Based** on the front page of the *Sun*, Paul would be collecting five bucks from Lester tonight. Just as he'd predicted, Dr. Bencher headlined the morning edition.

> Outside Dr. Gregory Bencher's office yesterday, protesters picketed his participation in a sexual molestation case. Inside the office, an unidentified assailant shot the psychiatrist dead. Police sources have identified the motive as robbery, denying a connection between the protest and the murder. No suspects have been arrested in the case.

Robbery? I hadn't intended to go by the bar this evening, but I couldn't wait to hear the latest on this turn of events.

I rolled into the Palm Lakes parking lot at seven, grateful, in spite of a sour stomach and a pounding headache, that I'd found the good sense somewhere to turn down

Al Geiberger, *Tempo. Harvey Penick's Little Red Book.* John Feinstein, *A Good Walk Spoiled.* And my personal favorite—Stephen Baker, *How to Play Golf in the Low 120s.* Cataloging Odell's collection was not why he'd left me in here, but I was at a loss for how to help Kaitlin. I was almost certain she'd made the cuts on her arm herself. I had no idea how to handle that. And I'd never mastered the skill needed to offer heartfelt condolences, never mind about a shrink who'd been murdered after persuading someone to file suit against her own father. Other possible topics of conversation seemed impossibly shallow, like golf, or even bigger minefields, like incest.

"I met your brother at Chili-Dippers last night," I finally blurted out.

"And he tried to talk you into asking me to drop the suit," she said. I shrugged. "I won't do it. Especially now that Dr. Bencher's dead. Someone tried to shut me up by killing Bencher, but it isn't going to work."

"You think he was murdered because of the lawsuit?"

"Maybe," she said. "Maybe it was those people Mother sicced on him—the False Memory Consociation. Fancy name for a bunch of cretins butting into business they know nothing about."

"You think they'd do something like that? While they're picketing right outside his door?"

"How the hell should I know what they would or wouldn't do," she said. "All I know is that he was the only one who believed me, and now he's dead."

"I'm sorry."

"Sure you're sorry," she said. "Everyone's sorry now. That doesn't help me live with it. Hearing his footsteps in the hall at night. All those games we played when I was little." Her voice had developed a girlish singsong quality. "Bouncing on his lap. A game for me. Masturbation for him."

"Do you have any ideas about who murdered Dr. Bencher? Did he have any enemies that you were aware of?"

"How will Bencher's death affect the lawsuit against your father?"

In spite of my instinctive dislike for this girl, I felt a rush of sympathy. The bright lights of the cameras washed her features out to shadows. With her eyes wide and her mouth open in confusion, she looked young and lost. Even so, I had to believe she would lash out at anyone who had the misguided urge to try to help her get her bearings.

Now there was a conflict a good shrink could seize upon. Unless, of course, your shrink was lying in the morgue with a bullet hole in his carotid artery.

I jumped in alarm when Odell tapped me on the shoulder. "Your junior clinic golfers are here," he said. "I'd suggest you start early and get them away from this zoo." I nodded, ashamed to be caught snooping.

I developed a hunch early on in the session that the seven kids Odell had me working with had been sprung from an expensive reform school just that morning. For the next hour, I was too busy to worry any more about either Kaitlin's dilemma or my own whopping failure as peer counselor.

"Swing it like a baseball bat," I told Angela, a chunky girl with pigtails and a broad band of freckles across her nose. "Slow it down at the top just long enough that a bird could sit and rest for a minute on your club. Then let her rip." Angela coiled up and belted a shot out past the fifty-yard marker. "Good girl," I said. "Now you're getting the hang of it!"

I left her to separate James and Joshua, twins with a death wish who were using their nine-irons to conduct a sword fight. They weren't bad kids, I had to remind my-

He offered Kaitlin a driver, a long, slender club with an enormous copper head and silvery-blue shaft. I strained to make out his now-whispered words. I thought I heard "Ball Hog," "Tee Warrior", and "Fairway Bruiser." Kaitlin laughed, shrugged off his hand, and accepted the club he offered. He stood behind her, arms folded, and watched as she clobbered a ball out into the field, well past any reasonable range where the drive of my dreams would have landed.

"Wow!" he said, pretending that the force of her swing had knocked him to the ground. She helped him to his feet, giggling, and brushed invisible debris off his backside with more meticulousness than the brief interaction with Astroturf seemed to merit. If I squinted hard enough, I could still make out the tic-tac-toe pattern of the cuts on her left arm. Hard to believe this was the same girl I'd seen crumpled up in Odell's office only a couple hours earlier. It seemed almost like theater. She had to know I was watching.

I hit a few shots with my short irons, working on the precise placement of my fingers on the club shaft. "Close the zipper and keep the hot dog in the bun" was how I described it to the kids this morning. I'd stoop to anything it took to bring the excruciating difficulty of the game down to their level. Or my own. Next I worked on keeping the tempo I'd tried to teach Angela. But my mind couldn't let go of the length of Kaitlin's drives. Or the sight of her running her hands over the Deikon rep's buttocks. From the wash of envy that followed both events, I guessed the long dry spell without a real boyfriend was beginning to wear me down. My few static-filled, long-distance phone conversations with Jack left a lot of needs unsatisfied.

I replaced the clubs in my bag. I'd have plenty of time to practice at the range in Florida. Besides that, if I didn't

Chapter 6

I pulled into the driveway behind Dave's pickup, surprised I didn't see him in the yard. After he finished his breakfast shift at Littles' By the Beach, you could usually count on finding him fussing over his domain: polishing the truck, sweeping pine straw off the roof of the house, or pulling interloping Spanish moss off the live oak that screened him from the neighbors on the left. This was a side of Dave I had to admire. Lord knows, hell, we all knew, he'd made a colossal mistake when he refused to sell out so they could build condos on our lot. Now ours was the only one-family home on the block. But damned if Dave let it bother him. He treated the property like it was a Rockefeller mansion, not an asbestos-shingled ranch in the middle of a tacky tourist zone.

I waved at Mrs. Driggers, who lived in the duplex next door and made our business her own. She could have played back the details of any fight the four families within her immediate jurisdiction had ever had. "Hey

wouldn't take a tip from me about where to buy a good sandwich.

"I really don't think I can help—"

"I want you to know, I never touched my baby," said Coach, before I could finish my sentence. His voice broke. "I'm so proud of her." Now he looked at Dave. "You know how it is with a daughter. She's the bright light in your life. You'd do anything for her. You'd never hurt her." He sat down hard, dropped his head in his hands, and let out what sounded to be a strangled sob.

My mind raced in a million directions. I doubted Dave could relate to anything Coach said. An expression of disgust flooded his face as soon as Coach mentioned "touch" and "baby." I flashed briefly on the memory of my own father. I doubted he could have related to Coach's misery, either—a man who'd left his daughter at a time when she needed him most. I pushed my thoughts away from Dad, and back toward Coach Rupert. I recalled a game we used to play as teenagers: Truth or Dare. Truth: Did you ever fondle your daughter?

Mom broke the painful silence. "I'm sure everything will work out just fine," she said, patting his knee awkwardly. My mother, master of the meaningless platitude.

"She needs help," said Coach Rupert. "And not from the likes of that asshole who screwed her up. I would have killed the bastard myself, if someone else hadn't beat me to it. She was fine before that. High-strung, yes. If anything, I should have paid more attention to her, not less."

"Leave it in God's hands," said Mom, still patting his knee. This was a new one on me. Mom didn't like to leave anything in anybody's hands, God included.

"That's why I came," said Coach. "Cassandra, I need your help. If only you could try and talk to her." He turned again to Dave. "We all have regrets about how we

ladling out stew to the recruits at some North Carolina
military base had anything to do with earning respect from
me.

Mom ushered Detective Maloney into the living room.

"If you don't mind," he said, looking at Mom and
Dave, "I'd like to speak to Miss Burdette alone." They
left the room, Mom moving slowly and watching back
over her shoulder, her forehead furrowed with worry.

"Chief thinks we need you to stay in the area until we
get a better handle on the Bencher case," he said. A day
that had already been plenty bad enough was now taking
a turn for the worse. My lips and tongue felt thick and
heavy. For a minute, I had trouble even getting my mouth
to form words.

"Please," I said. "This is my only shot, Detective.
Please don't take it away. I promise I'll stay in close
touch. It's only six days." He thought for several minutes,
then gave a small nod.

"I'm going to give you the phone number for Arthur
Pate at the Sarasota County sheriff's office. Call him as
soon as you get in. He can make sure we get a hold of
you if we need to." I nodded. "My ass is on the line here,
Cassandra. It's not protocol to allow anyone connected to
a murder case to leave the state in the middle of the investigation."

"Maybe you don't believe me," I said, "but I didn't do
it. I didn't even know the guy." He shrugged. I guessed
he'd heard that one before. "Thanks for letting me go."

The detective grimaced as he stood to leave. "One more
thing," he said. He paused, then smiled. "Hit 'em straight.
We could use a gal from Myrtle Beach on the Tour. Show
'em we don't just make golf courses, we know how to
play 'em, too."

I thanked him again and showed him to the door. Mom
reappeared the minute it slammed shut. From the syrupy

pushed to the back of the shelf, the taller ones poking up like dandelions through the carpet of fake fur.

Mom preferred to keep this room, like my relationship with her, firmly planted in the era when I was still ten years old. Well before I'd really gotten involved in what she called devil golf, before Charlie had pushed her away, and even before Dad had run off with Maureen. Maureen of the neon spandex and buns so tight she could send Morse code signals just by squeezing the muscles in her ass. I rubbed Cashbox behind the ears until he rumbled with satisfaction.

I lay down next to the cat and picked up the golf club I kept beside the bed. It was a Ben Hogan blade nine-iron, part of the hand-me-down set my father let me fool around with once I turned eight. I fit my fingers into the training grip I'd glued onto the end of the shaft, and flexed the club. I always thought more clearly with my hands in the proper overlapping position.

What had life really been like in the Rupert household? According to Kaitlin, Coach's so-called love for her had gone well past acceptable fatherly affection. His story, which couldn't have been more different, seemed a whole lot easier to believe. Was he capable of shooting the man who'd put those ideas in her head? Where was the fine line between loving a child too much and not nearly enough? In my case, Odell insisted that the reason my father stopped calling was because having just a little contact with me hurt more than having none at all. But all I felt was the gaping emptiness of his absence and the rage of my mother's blame. The phone rang downstairs, interrupting my gloomy ruminations.

"It's for you, dear," Mom called up the stairs. "It's Joe somebody."

"Hey, Doc," I said, picking up my pink Princess extension. "You won't even believe what's going on here." I

in that department. Forget all this and focus on your golf."

"Hah. Easier said than done. I can't wait for you to get to Venice. I need professional help. You, my friend, are just the man for the job."

"That's why I called," said Joe. I didn't like the note of sheepishness that had crept into his voice. "I'm not going to be able to get there until later in the week. Three guys withdrew from the PGA championship—that puts Mike in. I feel like I really need to be there with him. I'll try to get over to Venice on Thursday, Thursday night at the latest."

"Shit," I said. "Thursday is likely to be too late. You know the cut's on Wednesday."

"You know what to do, Cassie," he said. "And Laura will be there with you. I'm thinking it might even work out better if I'm not around—too many cooks spoiling the broth and all that."

"Fine," I said. "That's just great. Tell Mike to hit 'em straight. I'll see you later."

"Come on, Cassie . . ." I heard the pleading in his voice as I slammed down the phone.

against him. Even so, this guy's gravelly bark rated him one, with Katie Couric at ten, in terms of friendly first impressions.

"Pate here. I'll look for you at the Plantation this afternoon. Stick around until I find you."

The third message was Joe again. "I didn't get a chance to tell you that I've put in a couple calls to some friends about Bencher. I'll let you know what I hear. And remember what we've been talking about—don't worry about how you're playing on the practice rounds, you're just getting a mental picture of the layouts—" I punched delete. Son-of-a-rotten-bitch.

I knew Mike's first appearance in a major championship was a pivotal moment in his career. He could either handle the pressure well and set the table for even better performances in future majors, or choke, and color upcoming events in a negative way that would be difficult to override. You saw it over and over with golfers on the Tour. If they played well in one event, their confidence mounted and they tended to do well again the following year. Same with a big collapse—deep in some primitive part of the brain, the failure got connected with the tournament or golf course where it had occurred, making future wins there a lot less likely.

I also knew that since last summer, Mike had grown to rely on Joe. He hadn't said much about it, but I'd seen how Joe helped him get a grip on his nerves, and how that translated to his improved putting. If Joe could keep him from blowing up, no contest—anyone would rate that as more important than holding my hand through the Q-school practice rounds.

The bare-bones facts about Q-school were brutal. Hardly any of the girls who tried made it through to the LPGA Tour on their first attempt. From what I'd heard, you were supposed to learn a lot your first time out,

I pulled my rented Pontiac out onto Interstate 75. Even if I'd been set down blindfolded, I would have known instantly I was in South Florida. No mistaking the flat, flat landscape and shimmering heat. Not to mention my brand of haute cuisine at every rest stop—Waffle House and Cracker Barrel—homestyle Southern cooking that the rest of the country was just beginning to discover. I loved it here. After four years of college at UF, I called this crazy, mixed-up state loaded with retirees, itinerant wanderers, and rabid environmentalists my second home.

Forty-five minutes down the road, I arrived in Venice and at the Starlight Motel, recommended by the volunteers running Q-school and insisted on by Odell. "The week will be hard enough without spending the nights in some fleabag," he told me. "You pick some nice place and send the bill to me."

The lobby was big on "faux"—faux green marble floor, faux Impressionist paintings behind the desk, and a big island of faux palms decorated with café lights in the middle of the space. Even the desk clerk, with false eyelashes and Mary Kay foundation applied by trowel, seemed a little unreal. A young woman carrying her clubs arrived in the lobby just after I approached the counter. She and her mother were dressed in matching Liz Claiborne golf outfits. I watched them as the clerk processed my reservation.

"Look, Becky, they have a stamp machine right there," her mother said. The older woman pointed to a dispenser near the breakfast nook in the corner. "You can get that postcard to Daddy into the mail today." Why the hell would she be sending postcards from Q-school?

"Dear Daddy, Having a great time, wish you were here. Love, Becky"? Too weird.

I knew from the pit in my stomach that I felt bad about the mother thing too. Not that I'd want my own mother

desk. "You need to check in over there. We're in charge of all the volunteers. Let us know if we can help you in any way this week." Divot nodded vigorously. Little people named Bunker and Divot? I wondered if I'd walked into golf's version of *The Wizard of Oz*—I braced myself in case they burst into song. Or began a soft-shoe with their partners, Fairway and Chip Shot.

When no song and dance developed, I thanked the ladies and stepped in line behind two Asian women. One was in tears, the other argued in broken English for an exception to be made for her friend's lost application.

"That's why we spell it out on the form," said the woman behind the desk. She was dressed like a golfer— white polo shirt, khakis, sensible shoes, and a short hairstyle that would stand up to a brutal travel schedule and a parade of golf visors. She pointed to the paper in front of her and began to read aloud. " *'Late or incomplete entry not acceptable,'* " she said. " 'Deadline for entry means time of receipt at LPGA Headquarters. Entries should be submitted early to allow ample time for delay or error in transmission.' " The Asian player continued to sob. "I'm sorry," said the woman. "If the application turns up, you'll be able to play in the California tournament." Add *brisk* and *firm* to the list of adjectives that described her.

I was shaking when I approached the desk. "Cassandra Burdette." I offered her my sweating hand.

"Alice MacPherson," said the woman. The crushing handshake confirmed my first impression: no nonsense tolerated. Alice inclined her head in the direction of the weeping girl. "You feel bad about that, but there are rules." I nodded. "You're all set," she said, after pulling my record out of a stack of papers on her desk. "Here are the times we have available for practice rounds. For tournament play on Tuesday and Wednesday, you'll have one

against the bag stand and stretched. Hard to believe I was really here. Another piece of advice from Joe Lancaster came to mind.

"Try to stay away from thinking about the big picture," he'd said. "Your mind can run on a thousand tracks, but your body can only reasonably handle one shot at a time. So, when I ask what you're thinking, I don't want to hear, 'How am I going to beat all these girls who are better prepared than me and have more experience and who will probably kick my ass and ruin my dream of competing on the Ladies Professional Golf Tour?' Okay?"

I'd laughed hard when he put it that way a couple of weeks ago. Today, that run-on thought was as real as the grass in front of me, and not the least bit funny. I couldn't stop thinking about the Asian girl, whose chances for qualifying this week had been torpedoed by the U.S. Mail. Or maybe, to give the mail service the benefit of the doubt, some office clerk had screwed up and misplaced her application. Ouch. Or, suppose the girl's ambivalence about competing had subconsciously sabotaged her to the point where she "accidentally" threw the thing out herself. I laughed. I'd obviously spent too damn much time lately in the presence of headshrinkers.

I pulled out my wedge and set up to hit short pitch shots to a red flag fifty yards out in the range. I wasn't going to make the cut as a long ball hitter, if Kaitlin was representative of the other players in the field. I'd have to depend on accurate approach shots and lots of putts dropping. After shanking two balls out to the right, I put the wedge away and retreated to easy swings with my nine-wood. It was hard to hit a bad shot with a club that forgave almost anything.

"Your backswing looks a little flat."

Some poor chump getting last-minute advice, I thought. Let's hope it helps.

"So. You're the little gal they think offed that head-shrinker." He handed me my club.

"No." I wiped the sheriff's sweat off the grip of the nine-wood. "I'm the one who found him after he'd been shot."

"You don't 'specially look like a cold-blooded killer." He hitched his trousers up until they almost covered the stretch of stomach and undershirt that had escaped while he swung.

"I didn't—"

"Maybe a crime of passion," said the sheriff. "Yeah, that looks like more your style. Say you asked the doctor out for a drink and he says he's married. Then you don't want to take no for an answer so you push harder and he still says no. So you shoot 'im. Maybe you didn't think it out ahead of time, you're just hot-blooded, that's all." His eyes swept over my entire body, stopping to linger on my chest and just below my waist. "Or maybe he didn't say no. Those doctors all have couches in their offices, don't they? Just waiting for the pretty girls. Then he felt bad later about acting unprofessional and called off the whole thing. And then you shot 'im."

"I did not know the man." I spoke the words slowly, as if to a very young child or a mentally retarded person, trying to hold the fury and fear out of my voice.

He continued on as if I'd said nothing. "We know it couldn't have been a professional job. No hired gun worth his salt is gonna shoot some guy in the throat. Too messy, first of all. Second, might not really finish the job. Guy could talk or signal something on his way out. Know what I'm sayin'?"

What was he saying? It was hard to tell from his demeanor whether he considered me a serious suspect or just enjoyed playing with me, knowing he had me trapped. "I guess maybe I don't know what you mean," I said.

Chapter 8

I packed up and left the range as soon as Sheriff Pate's squad car pulled away. I planned to stop at the Publix supermarket I'd passed on the way to the club, buy a few staples to stock my kitchenette, and retreat to the motel. From there, my plan consisted of blotting out my mounting anxiety with bad TV sitcoms and a six-pack of Busch beer.

I browsed the frozen food section in Publix and selected black bean burritos, well within my budget at three for a dollar. Then I moved to the produce section for a few bananas. Becky, of the postcard-to-Daddy fame, was there with her mother, who pushed a shopping cart loaded with strawberries, yams, melons, and broccoli. Sure, rub it in. Mommy was going to serve home-cooked meals all week so Becky didn't get gas or otherwise feel uncomfortable as she stood over her important putts. I glanced down at the frozen lumps in my carry basket, then abandoned them in front of the beer cooler and checked out with just the

and sunny concern for the well-being of random customers.

Halfway into my second Corona, I felt a tap on my shoulder. "Penny for your thoughts, Cassie. You're looking very serious tonight. As well as lovely, I cannot help but add," said Gary Rupert. It took me just a moment to recognize him, then I felt a rush of relief and gratitude for a familiar face. Any familiar face.

"You startled me," I said. "I didn't expect to see anyone I knew in here. Have a seat. You're down here to watch Kaitlin?"

"I'm her caddie," said Gary. "I thought you knew that."

"Lucky her," I said. "You don't see my brother out here with me." I felt disloyal even mentioning Charlie. He supported me the best he could, considering his own pressure-cooker career as junior partner in a big D.C. law firm. "How'd you get the time off?"

"At the moment, I've got all the time in the world," he said. "I made the mistake of signing on with a dot-com last year. They did a great selling job—I was going to make a million before I hit thirty-five. Instead, they hit the skids and I'm on the street."

"Sore subject, I guess. But good timing for Kaitlin."

We chatted about our respective trips down and places we'd found to stay. The Ruperts had rented a condo on the Bobcat's eighteenth fairway—"Kaitlin wanted to be close in," Gary explained. He looked hard at me. "How are you holding up?"

I sighed. "Rough day."

"Practice didn't go well?"

"There's that, though I hardly got any in, really. The worst is this business about Bencher's murder." I told him about my meeting with Sheriff Pate.

"So he thinks the murderer might believe you know something about how Bencher was killed?" I nodded. "Like what?"

lin's not really so bad, you know," he added. "She's just mega-insecure. In her mind, everyone's a threat. Especially a woman as talented and attractive as you."

His hand brushed a little farther up my thigh, maybe accidental, maybe not. In any case, the combination of alcohol, Gary's concern and compliments, and the feel of his touch on my leg was surprisingly pleasant. I tried to think why I'd been so definite about refusing a date with him ten years ago. Just a dumb, shallow teenager, I decided. Drawing conclusions based on how clear someone's complexion was or how many touchdowns they scored. Attributes which didn't mean too much at this stage of life. Then I decided that if he touched my leg again, even farther up the thigh, I would not remove his hand.

Kaitlin's arrival at the bar truncated any further development. She had her Deikon rep in tow, radiating an odd combination of testosterone and bonhomie.

"I hope I'm not interrupting something," she said. The unpleasant curl of her lip suggested the opposite.

"Hi, sis," said Gary. "I'd just about given up on you. I'm starving. Have you met Walter Moore, Cassie?"

"Yo." My hand disappeared briefly into the Deikon equipment hunk's fleshy palm.

"Want to join us for dinner?" said Gary.

One quick look at the expression on Kaitlin's face made it clear just how unwelcome I would be at the Rupert dinner party. "I'll stay where I am, thanks. I'm sure my order's just about ready to come up," I said. "How'd you make out today, Kaitlin? Hit 'em straight?" That said just for the annoyance value of making her acknowledge my presence.

"Just fine."

"It's common courtesy to ask, 'And you?' " Gary said.

do both come from Myrtle Beach. And I wouldn't mind having her talent off the tee, but any similarity stops there."

Mary laughed. "She hasn't made a lot of friends out on Futures. If she wins, she's unbearable. When she loses, she's worse."

"The only things she's really interested in talking about are her golf game and this false memory business," said Adele. "We're people, too. Even if you don't want to be best friends, you could at least make a little conversation. How're you doing? Where're you from? Are you married or happy?" I laughed, thinking of Gary insisting that Kaitlin ask about my day.

"It's worse than that," said Eve. "She's mean. Things don't go her way, she lashes out at whoever's in her path."

"And don't forget calling people on obscure rules in the USGA book. She's called girls on teeing up ahead of the markers, using tees as ball-markers, the two-ball rule, you name it. She's never heard of giving the benefit of the doubt," added Adele.

"The low point was a match play tournament when Kaitlin's opponent chipped in for bird and Kaitlin insisted she replay the shot because she was away," said Eve. "By the letter of the law, she was correct, but the spirit was mean. It really took the heart out of the girl she was playing."

"She's always correct," said Mary. "But what gets to you is the steady drip, drip, drip of her self-righteousness. Most of us avoid her like the plague."

"Except for Julie," corrected Eve.

"Who's Julie?" I asked.

"It's a long story," said Mary. "Short version, Julie Atwater seems to be Kaitlin's new best friend. Long version, we think Kaitlin talked her into accusing her own father of incest a couple of months ago."

made the acquaintance of some friendly faces, but at the same time, I felt desperate to get off by myself and re-group. I hoped for an inspirational and sexy phone mes-sage from Jack Wolfe. I also wanted to talk to Joe. I just wasn't sure I was quite ready to forgive his defection.

"I'm going to hit the hay," I said, standing and sliding a twenty-dollar bill onto the table. "I'm beat."

"Sure you don't want to go clubbing with us?" Eve demonstrated an abbreviated funky chicken.

"Thanks anyway, big date tomorrow. My first encoun-ter with the Panther."

I made my way back through the bar, which was now crowded, noisy, and smoky. I caught sight of Gary Rupert sitting at a stool on the far side of the room, but I'd had enough conversation for one night with him as well. It wasn't until I was buckling the seat belt in my rental car that it occurred to me how familiar the man talking with him looked. Something about the broad shoulders and slightly thinning hair.

I drove back to my motel, wishing I could get Sheriff Pate's warning out of my mind. Even worrying about dou-ble bogeys on the four holes that comprised the Panther's Claw would be preferable to imagining the possibility of being stalked for information I did not possess. I thought back over the evening. I decided to put any feelings about Gary, sexual or otherwise, on hold. His sweet defense of Kaitlin reminded me of my own brother, Charlie. Charlie would stick up for me no matter what the circumstances. In this case, Gary had to be off the mark. From all that my dinner companions reported, Kaitlin didn't have much going that could be sincerely defended. In fact, I didn't have to stretch far to picture her, in my place, in the ugly scenario Sheriff Pate had described—a crime of passion gone sour. Disappointment twisted into murder. For what it was worth, I'd run that by Pate tomorrow.

At 6:30, I bought a copy of the *Herald-Tribune* in the lobby. I planned to shroud myself in the paper and fend off potential chitchat with traveling salesmen about the latest tip from *Golf Digest* on how to get out of a sand bunker. I loaded my tray with orange juice from concentrate, anemic-looking coffee, corn flakes, and a chocolate-covered donut that had seen fresher days. Becky's mom was probably whipping up a whites-only, veggie omelet and a fresh fruit salad while Becky lounged in bed watching cartoons.

I skimmed a small article on the front page of the *Tribune:* LPGA SECTIONAL QUALIFIER RETURNS TO PLANTATION GOLF AND COUNTRY CLUB. The writer described how the future stars of the LPGA generally scrapped their way through Q-school and onto the professional golf Tour right here in Venice, Florida. It certainly wasn't news, but the facts in black and white caused my heart to rev up in what had to be an unwholesome way. At the end of the article, the reporter interviewed the club manager about the unusually strong presence of protesting pickets at Futures Tour venues over the last half year.

"This is a sporting event, not a political debate or a circus. We will absolutely not tolerate any disruption of that kind at this tournament," insisted Manager Jones. "These people have been put on notice."

Kaitlin's Deikon dude appeared next to me with his tray of breakfast food.

"Yo. Mind if I join you? It's Lassie, isn't it?"

"Cassie," I said. I knew I needed a haircut, but really, a collie? Jesus, this guy was a dope. And I did mind if he joined me, but with his buns already hitting the wrought-iron café chair across from me, I saw no gracious way out. So I folded up the paper and pulled my tray

so the technical guys can measure her club head speed and the torque she puts on the shaft. As far as I'm concerned, she's got the template for a nearly perfect swing." He laughed. "Perfect body, too, but don't tell her I said that. She'll get the PC police after me." I waited for him to comment about how he'd like to measure the torque she put on *his* shaft, too.

He grinned as if reading my mind. Peculiar twitching movements had begun to march up the side of his neck and into his jawline. This guy seemed clearly head-over-heels in love, but laced with an Oil Can Boyd kind of just-about-tipped-over-the-edge intensity.

"But, hey, listen, that club, the Ball Hog or whatever we end up calling it, it's not out yet," Walter said, dropping his voice to a low rumble. "I'm not supposed to be using it for demo. My ass would be grass. So do me a favor and keep it under your hat, okay?" I nodded. "Hey, have a fantastic day," he said, cramming the last half of a bran muffin into his mouth. "I got places to do and things to be."

"Catch you later then, dude," I said. I watched him lunge out of the delicate chair and jam the contents of his tray into the trash. *Hunk* was the only way to describe him—muscles that made every Deikon logo on his clothing quiver. But Lord, what a moron.

Back in the motel room, I dialed into my cell phone voice mail. Joe had left the first message the night before. "I hope you're not still ticked off. I'm at Sawgrass. Mike's a mess. I'm trying to hold him together, but it may take every bottle of Elmer's glue and roll of Scotch tape they have in Ponte Vedra. His new caddie doesn't have your magic touch. I'll get over as soon as I can, but it could be Thursday. Call me tonight. By the way, before he was killed, Bencher was up to his eyebrows fighting the False Memory outfit. They had him targeted for harassment. He

went into your choice." According to him, you couldn't just stumble into something—everything you did or said had some deeper meaning. Hah!

Two Asian women introduced themselves to me on the path to the tee. Sachiko was blocky and masculine. Hiroko was so delicate I couldn't imagine she had the strength to swing a full-length driver. Neither one spoke much English. I was able to make out that they were Japanese, had spent the last year competing on the Asian Tour but had not met Jack Wolfe, and not much else. Hiroko introduced me to her mother, who was even smaller than her daughter. She carried an enormous silver umbrella to shade herself from the Florida August sun. She was dressed in exquisite golf clothing, down to white anklets with pink pom-poms and spiked Lady Fairway silver saddle shoes. Perhaps she was poised to take her daughter's place in the event of an emergency.

Divot, one of the volunteer Munchkins I'd met yesterday, greeted us on the first tee.

"How are you girls doing?" she asked.

"Great," I said. "We haven't hit a single ball yet, so no chance to get into trouble." The Japanese women laughed.

"You may find the greens a bit fast," said Divot. "An underground water pipe burst two days ago. Our irrigation system is out of commission until they get the replacement part from Miami. We're dreadfully sorry for any inconvenience."

As we set off down the first fairway, there was little sign of the tension that I knew would dominate the first round of the tournament. Like the other girls, I could repeat any shot that didn't meet my standards. Today I was under no obligation to accept balls hooked out of bounds, putts missed on either side of a hole, skulled chips, balls in the water, or any other missteps with ugly consequences. I added my own descriptive notes to the LPGA

Beach. He probably hadn't seen a shower stall or laundromat since then either. The other protesters were strangers. This time the signs read: "Whatever Happened to 'Honor Thy Father'?" and "Mythical Memories Cause Real Pain." I had to assume their presence was related to Kaitlin's suit. It was hard to see how she could concentrate on golf with that much ruckus around her.

I skirted around the crowd, delivered the cart to the maintenance area and my bag to my car trunk, and headed back to the putting green. Maybe if I sank a hundred short ones this afternoon, I could avoid a full-blown panic over a must-have putt during Tuesday's or Wednesday's round.

After half an hour, I started to get a rhythm going. I felt comfortable with my left-hand low grip, which I'd revamped just a month ago, and developed an eye for the subtle breaks in the green. I focused on Joe Lancaster's putting credo: Visualize the relaxation flowing down my arms and into the putter. Putter and arms are one.

"Miz Burdette, do you have a minute?" said the gravelly voice of Sheriff Pate. Polite of him to put it that way, but I knew chatting with him wasn't really a choice. I picked up my balls and followed him to the scanty shade of a palm tree.

The sheriff looked frazzled and hot. His shirttails had come loose from his pants, and a wide band of dark sweat striped the length of his back. "Let's return, if we may, to the scene of Dr. Bencher's office," he said. "Explain again why you were there." I repeated what I'd told the first police officer on the scene, then Detective Maloney, then Pate himself, just yesterday.

"I understand you were visiting with the doctor next door," said Pate. "What I want to understand is why."

"It was my regular appointment," I said. "I generally see Dr. Baxter on Thursdays."

I sighed. I could feel and smell the perspiration dampening a wide circle under the arms of my golf shirt. I breathed in deeply and focused on the horizontal lines of the clubhouse across the street. When I felt calm enough to speak, I repeated the story of finding Bencher lying behind his desk. In spite of Pate's barrage of questions about what I might have seen or heard, I had nothing new to add.

"It's been nice talkin' to you. I'll see you tomorrow," said Pate, returning my putter. He left me under the palm, angry and wilted.

touch with Pate," he said. "Those were the conditions under which we allowed you to leave the state."

"I know that," I said. "But you didn't say he would be harassing me. How's the case really coming?"

"No suspects arrested," he said. "That's all I can tell you. Do you want to file a formal complaint against Pate?"

I considered this. Pate was plenty mean already. Filing a complaint would be like poking a sleepy rattlesnake with a nine-iron.

"No. Thanks anyway." Thanks for nothing, I thought as I hung up. Then I decided to call Joe. I'd nursed my grudge long enough. Now I needed his advice.

"You've reached the voice mail of Dr. Joe Lancaster. I can't take your call right now, but leave your name and number and I'll be happy to get back to you. Meanwhile, keep your head down and have fun out there!"

I left a message asking him to call and then stretched out on the bed to think. I pictured Joe out on the practice green with Mike, where I should have been. Where Joe should have been with me. Where I *would* have been, Joe or no Joe, were it not for Pate's annoying interruption. From all appearances, the police had not made much progress in solving the murder. Either Pate still thought I had reason to kill Bencher, or he believed I had seen or heard something that would identify the actual killer. Or he got a buzz on by throwing his status around and knocking me off balance. Regardless of the reason, I was sick of our little conversations. I saw one way to get that ape off my back: look into the Bencher situation myself. Joe wouldn't approve of this plan, but he hadn't had to sit through two miserable sessions with Pate, with more tête-à-têtes looming the rest of the week.

I pulled out the phone book and looked up Will Turner, the head honcho of the False Memory Consolation. In

At first, the conversation centered on golf. We all agreed that the Panther greens verged on the edge of suicidally fast, and that the volunteers were sweet, the sandhill cranes aggressive, and the fairways in excellent condition. If any of these girls lacked confidence or harbored other unpleasant feelings about the week ahead, they showed no sign of it. Nicki went to the small kitchen and returned with a plate of Oreos and a pitcher of grape juice.

"Let's get started," said Joanne, a plump, dark-haired girl with an eerie resemblance to Rosie O'Donnell. "Our scripture reading tonight is from Romans, chapter one, verses eighteen to thirty-two." She opened her Bible and read a passage about the many faces of ungodliness, homosexuality prominent among them. It didn't look like it was going to be difficult to steer the subject in the direction I needed it to go. Joanne finished reading and prayed that we could all live as Paul had instructed us to do. Then she and Nicki went through the Bible verses line by line, explaining how we were to apply them to our lives.

"As I see it, Paul condemned the Greeks for a lifestyle of debauchery and self-satisfaction. He expected them, and us by extension, to live a God-centered life instead. Any questions?" Joanne inquired. The group sat silent and smiling.

I took my second plunge of the evening. "I know I have a lot to learn," I said. "I'm a part-time Presbyterian with barely a leaf-through familiarity with the Bible." Two of the other students giggled. "But you seem to be saying that we should interpret what you've read to us quite literally."

Nicki and Joanne exchanged glances. "It's the word of God," said Nicki, holding her hands out in an expression of heavenly acceptance. Joanne clutched the Bible to her chest and bobbed her head in support.

women often enough to know it was a path I'd prefer to avoid.

The group leaders rose from their seats and came to sit on the couch on either side of me. "You are doing the right thing," said Nicki. "We'll help you."

"I didn't mean me. . . ."

Joanne put her arm around my shoulder and squeezed hard. I could smell the icing on her breath as she whispered to me. "The first step is to confess your sins before the Lord. You must not give in to the devil's temptation."

"I wasn't talking about my issues," I said. "I'm worried about a friend who seems to have started down this path. She's changed a lot recently." I hesitated. "She has family problems."

"Ah," said Joanne. "A friend who has been misled by the smooth words of the devil. Could it be Julie Atwater?" I lowered my eyes, then nodded.

"Satan circulates among us on this earth," said Nicki sternly. "Sometimes he takes the form of a woman. Julie met the devil and was persuaded to follow his ways." I figured she had to be talking about Kaitlin. Who did have a bit of the devil in her, as far as I was concerned.

"Wasn't that Julie's father I saw marching today at the club?" I asked.

"The Lord told Mr. Atwater he must seek to destroy the devil wherever he finds him," said Joanne. "Whether that be in his own daughter or wherever he chooses to make his presence known. Mr. Atwater is a true soldier of the Lord." Her admiration of what appeared to me to be unreasoned fanaticism raised a warning crop of goose bumps on my chest and arms.

To my enormous relief, the meeting broke up shortly after this discussion. I thanked the girls for their hospitality and comfort and bolted from the condo. The moon had risen during the meeting and now cast long, serrated

tournament and my clumsy detective work had hardened my back and shoulder muscles into stony knots.

Gary returned in several minutes with two Rolling Rocks. We sat down with our backs against the bark of a live oak and drank. The moon gleaming through wisps of Spanish moss made a checkerboard of shadows on his face, softening the sharp contour of his nose and smoothing the roughness in his skin. We chatted about the day, the golf courses, the thunderstorms predicted for the following afternoon. By the time I'd finished my beer, the tightness had begun to ebb from my neck muscles. Gary took the empty bottle from my hand, then leaned over and kissed me. He broke away as quickly as he'd leaned in.

"I'm glad we got that over with. It was ten years overdue," he said. "But maybe we can talk more back in Myrtle. You've got enough going on already this week. Have a good night, pal. Good luck tomorrow." He stood up, collected both empties, and walked back in the direction of his condo.

What in the hell was all that about? I wondered, as I stumped back to my car. Now I'd developed a pounding headache, as well as new knots in every muscle above my waist. Gary was right: a romantic interlude had no place in a week already too full. And he didn't know the half of what I was into. So why in the bloody hell had he even brought it up?

I listened to my new phone messages before leaving the motel. The first was from Mom. I remembered, with the usual surge of guilt, that I hadn't called her since arriving in Florida.

No greeting, just a tremulous voice. "Max Harding came into the restaurant for lunch yesterday. He's so handsome. He asked how the week was going for you. I told him he would have to call you himself, because even though I'm your mother I would certainly have no idea. Love you." And she hung up. The second message was not much better.

"This is Pate. I'm busy at the office today and can't get out to the club. Stop by the sheriff's department when you're finished this afternoon. Take 41 toward downtown Venice, turn at State Road 776, we're on the left." Great, just what I needed, a command appearance from the grand buffoon. I left the motel in a nasty funk.

I grabbed a banana and a cheese Danish as I entered the dining area at the country club, then found a seat at a table with Mary Morrison and Eve Darling. Mary pointed out Julie Atwater, who chatted with Kaitlin several tables in front of us. I would not have guessed from Julie's perfectly made up face and cheerful façade that she had a major feud going on with her dad and the Bible study group. Not to even mention inner conflict.

The deputy commissioner of the LPGA started the meeting off by introducing Alice and the other LPGA staff in attendance, then the head honcho of the Plantation Country Club. We clapped politely for each of them.

"There will be two waves of tee times on both courses tomorrow and Wednesday, at seven-thirty and eleven A.M.," the commissioner explained. "As you know, a random draw will determine your pairings. After Wednesday, half the field will be cut, with the remaining golfers arranged in threesomes according to their cumulative

laughed. That seemed an obvious and gratuitous reminder, but I knew how common sense could completely evaporate in tense tournament conditions.

"Third, a list of nonconforming equipment is posted on the bulletin board. The use of one of these drivers in USGA competitions is the grounds for disqualification. Finally, your practice balls are provided courtesy of Titleist. They'll be donated to junior girls' golf programs after this week. They're very nice balls, but please don't take them home. We get very upset if they disappear into your bag." The girls at my table laughed again.

"Only thirty of you will go on to the final round of the LPGA Q-school. As far as we're concerned, you're all winners. Play your best and good luck." The tears that sprang to my eyes surprised me. It was really happening. I was no longer lying home on that gingham bedspread, looking at the posters of Nancy Lopez and Freddie Couples holding their trophies, dreaming that one day I'd be there, too. This was my chance: I promised myself to enjoy every minute of it. Okay, at least some of them, I bargained.

Before heading over to the Bobcat course, I called Dr. Turner's office. His receptionist was delighted to offer me an appointment the same afternoon at five P.M. She was probably afraid she wouldn't get a paycheck this month if she didn't book a few more suckers into his schedule. I'd have time to pick Laura up at the airport and still make my pseudo-session with Turner.

"May I ask your chief complaint?" the receptionist said. "You certainly aren't required to tell me this on the phone, but it does help the doctor prepare for you."

I vacillated for a moment about how much to say. I already regretted having given my real name. "I'd rather not. . . . I'm not really comfortable. . . ."

hadn't expressed the slightest interest in caddying, probably wasn't even aware I was competing at Q-school. Buck up. It could be worse. He could be Leviticus.

"Aren't you from Myrtle Beach?" asked Julie on the ride over to the first tee. I nodded. "Kaitlin's mentioned you."

"I don't like the sound of that," I said. "Whatever she said, puh-leeze give me the benefit of the doubt."

"It's not that bad," she said with a smile that struck me as sincere. "She doesn't have me brainwashed or anything." She pointed to the players in front of us reaching the first green. "Looks like we're good to go here."

I watched as the other two players hit their drives, Jessica's long and straight, Julie's a wicked slice that dribbled into a bunker on the right side of the fairway.

"Damn it," she said. "I must be swinging over the top."

I hit a pop-up fly straight down the middle, though barely past the hundred-and-fifty-yard marker. I joined Julie in the cart for the ride to my ball. Next I skimmed a seven-iron low and ugly down the fairway. Julie stepped on the gas when I'd barely sat down and we lurched toward the green. Once there, Jessica sank a three-footer for birdie and slapped hands with her father. Julie and I both three-putted for bogeys.

"Number two's a beast," I heard Jessica tell her father as she got into the cart. "With my draw, I'm either in the mounds or the trap. The approach to the green's even worse."

"You gotta love it, though, honey," said her father, replacing her putter in the bag. "Just being here—what a dream come true." She hugged him before he trotted off toward the next hole. It was going to take every bit of mental toughness I owned to finish this round without feeling pathetic.

I got out of the cart to stretch. "Bencher helped you figure some stuff out?"

"I only saw the doctor once," said Julie. She wiped the perspiration off her forehead with her golf towel, then waved it in the direction of the clubhouse. "Those idiots with placards want you to believe that there's no such thing as an honest memory. Evil and persuasive shrinks plant thoughts into the weak shells of the women who come for help. In my case, Bencher barely said a word. It was like all this garbage had been bubbling inside me and it took fifty minutes of spewing it out in his office to figure out what I'd been thinking and feeling. You know what I mean?"

"I think so. Just having someone listen sometimes helps you put words to what's in the back of your mind."

Julie nodded. "I knew for a long time that there was something wrong with my relationship with my father. Some of the things he did . . ." She looked first as though she might cry, then she pulled her lips into a thin line and narrowed her eyes. "But I didn't want to see this too clearly—who wants to think their father is a lech?"

"Obviously, I don't know you very well, but you seem so different from him."

"He and Mom split up when I was eight so I've seen very little of him since then. Trust me, there was a good reason Mom dumped him. The better question is why she married him in the first place."

"So Bencher didn't suggest he'd abused you?"

"No. The only thing he commented on specifically was how my father had hurt me emotionally. Dr. Bencher was quite clear about that."

I glanced up toward the green. Two of the three players ahead had dropped their balls outside the hazard and were preparing to chip on. "Do you mind saying how?"

We finished the remainder of the round without further conversation, other than "nice shot" or, following a number of my unfortunate skirmishes with the water, the woods, and the rough, "tough luck." Nothing seemed to be working. I pulled out the note card listing swing thoughts I'd worked on with Joe and Odell back at the Palm Lakes driving range. These short phrases were to be used to help clear messages from mind to body that interfered with a smooth swing.

"Don't get too technical," Joe had told me. "Your body knows very well what to do. Your mind has to let go, get out of the way, and let your body do its job."

Whispering "Let it go" produced a snap hook out of bounds on five. Using "Let it flow," I popped two balls in the water on six. By the time we reached the eighteenth green, where Gary had watched me pantomime my putt last night, I was more over par than I even wanted to count.

"Lucky thing you got that out of your system," said Jessica. "Good luck tomorrow, girls."

I turned in my cart and prepared to head north to Pate's office and the airport. My cell phone vibrated, letting me know I'd received a message while out on the golf course.

"Cassie, it's Jack. Sorry I missed you. The time difference is killing me. Good luck tomorrow, Gorgeous, and don't let anyone tell you Budweiser isn't in your training regimen. Have one on me. Let me know how it's going. Take care."

I whistled all the way to Sarasota.

"Fine, thanks." I sure as hell wasn't going to discuss my golf problems with this bozo.

"Any new thoughts about Bencher?"

"Honest to God, Sheriff Pate," I said. "I'm doing my best to forget about Bencher. I told you everything I possibly knew. I even made up a few extra details just to make you happy." I could see he didn't find my little joke at all funny.

"This is serious, Miz Burdette. A man's been killed here."

"I'm well aware of that, sir. You may remember that I found him."

"Then until we solve the case and determine that you in fact were not involved, I'd suggest you do your best to cooperate."

"I'm trying." I didn't want to cry in front of Pate, but it was going to take all the willpower I had to hold back the frustrated tears.

"I'll look for you over at the Plantation tomorrow," he said. "They may need some extra protection if the protests continue." He sighed as if it were a great burden to have so much responsibility.

"That's it? I'm free to go?" Pate nodded. I left the building, again infuriated and confused by the man's interrogation. Today, I couldn't discern any real reason for him to have asked me in.

I felt better the instant I saw the round face and sturdy fireplug shape of Laura Snow getting off the plane. She insisted her size was a by-product of her combination Eastern European peasant and Choctaw heritage, and that it brought many advantages—not the least being a low center of gravity, useful for weathering windstorms and balancing golf swings. In addition, Laura brimmed with

Dr. Turner's waiting room was plainer than the one shared by Baxter and Bencher. Metal chairs with thin, blue vinyl cushions lined the walls. A faded travel poster featuring the Eiffel Tower hung above the secretary's desk. If I had to wait long, there wouldn't be much to distract me from counting the fast thumping of my heartbeats.

"I'm here to see Dr. Turner. I'm Cassandra Burdette," I told the receptionist.

"He's tied up with some unexpected business. You can have a seat over there." She flipped her long blond braid over her shoulder and waved at the metal seats in the corner of the room. I sat and paged through the latest issue of *My Self* magazine. While I read "Cheapo Beauty Buys That Will Take Ten Years Off Your Face," the secretary painted her nails purple. During "The Single Best Diet for Your Abs," she lined her eyelids with silver and applied three coats of mascara. I couldn't help staring as she began dabbing at her cleavage with cotton balls dipped in two separate colors of liquid foundation.

"It's the new thing," she explained when she caught me gawking. "The shadows fool the eye into thinking there's more there than is actually the case."

I smiled. To me it appeared that her gifts in that department were bountiful to begin with. Through the connecting office door, I heard voices raised in heated conversation. The secretary lifted her shoulders in an apologetic shrug, outlined her lips in magenta, then filled them in with glossy pink. When I could no longer stand sitting still, I got up and began to pantomime my putting stroke.

"Are you here for that golf tournament?" the secretary asked.

"Yes," I said. "Qualifying school."

"I can't promise too much, but I could certainly call over and get you a grounds pass to the tournament for the weekend. Maybe Mike would introduce you after the round is finished on Saturday. The guys aren't always in the most social mood, though. A lot depends on how the day went." I knew damn well I was leading her on. Mike Callahan would no more consent to playing matchmaker than put on a pair of culottes and tee off on the women's Tour. Though he definitely had the legs for it.

"Oh, wait 'til my girlfriends hear about this! They'll be absolutely green. Let me give you my home phone so you can tell me what you were able to set up." Distributing her still-tacky nails carefully around a purple pen, she wrote out her name and number in looping script and offered it to me. "Oh, my God, what do you think I should wear?"

"As you can see," I said, gesturing to my baggy khaki shorts and navy blue golf shirt, "I'm not part of the fashion vanguard. I choose clothes strictly for comfort and the size of their pockets. And I really can't speak for Rick's taste."

"Oh, he definitely dresses preppie. Haven't you seen him in the Polo ads? He looks so cute with his hair slicked back!"

I laughed. "I know you'll come up with something nice. That magazine"—I pointed to where I'd been sitting— "says the trend is to show skin, but not necessarily cleavage. I guess bare breasts are considered cliché this year. So what does that leave? Halter tops? Short shorts?" I hated to egg her on with sleazy suggestions, but if you wanted to stand out from the pack of golf groupies in the gallery, there was an awful lot of competition.

"Oh, my God, how could I ever repay you?"

"Well, maybe you could help me with something. I came to talk to Dr. Turner about the False Memory Con-

ready to wrap things up." I heard two doors slam from inside Turner's office.

"Let me give you my cell phone number in case you think of anything else." I handed her a scrap torn off the paper she'd given me. "And I'll call you about the tournament this weekend."

"Miss Burdette?" A tall man with a thin mustache peered out of the office. He wore gray polyester slacks, pilled around the pockets and the seat, and a white short-sleeved shirt so thin I could see the outline of his muscle T-shirt underneath, along with a crop of bushy black chest hair. Definitely a candidate for the fashion "don'ts" column of *My Self* magazine.

"I'm Dr. Turner. Please come in. You can go home now, Jeanine," he said to the secretary. He frowned. "I thought I told you to leave at five." Jeanine scraped the beauty products off her desk into the top drawer and scurried out of the room.

Turner's inner office was as plain as the waiting area. Metal filing cabinets covered one wall; bookshelves piled with masses of papers lined the other side. The desk was crowded with a computer, fax machine, scanner, and more stacks of papers and files. Nothing at all on the walls.

"Have a seat," he said, indicating twins of the metal chairs I'd seen in the outer office. "Sorry about the wait. Sorry about the mess. We just moved in a couple of weeks ago and I haven't got things sorted out." His forehead wrinkled in concentration. "Miss Peters said you wished to discuss a possible family problem with me. Tell me about that."

"I've been in counseling." My voice came out in a squeak. "When I told my mother some of the things I'd been remembering, she begged me to come to talk to you before anything else. . . . Before I confronted my father." Now my voice shook with what I hoped was a reasonable

Dr. Turner shook his head sadly. "Lots of reasons. Sometimes it's just naïveté, sometimes people are incompetent, sometimes it's zealotry, or greed."

"Sometimes they must be right," I said.

"Of course. But let me be perfectly blunt with you, Cassandra, trauma therapy means a long recovery. And a long recovery means a steady income."

"You mean he told me that those things happened to keep me coming to my sessions?" I opened my eyes wide in what I hoped looked like shocked disbelief. Which wasn't difficult—I *was* shocked. Did shrinks really keep their customers coming just for the income? What about Baxter? Was the frequency of my appointments based on the projected level of his retirement fund?

"It's possible," said Dr. Turner. I had to remind myself that we weren't talking about Dr. Baxter here. We were trashing a made-up shrink, a hypothetical man without scruples who'd taken advantage of a vulnerable and confused young woman. "I could help more if you'd be willing to describe what your treatment has been like. Did your counselor use memory recovery techniques?"

"He didn't call it that," I said. "What does that mean?"

"There are a number of techniques which allow these people to suggest or implant memories that did not really occur. Hypnosis, massage therapy to uncover body memories, sodium amytyl injections, to name a few." The sneer in his voice was unmistakable.

"I guess I had hypnosis. My counselor said he would take me back to those years so I could remember things I'd forgotten. I don't know what to think. I'm so confused." Now would have been a good time to squeeze a few tears out or at least a few distressed whimpers, but I was afraid Dr. Turner's bullshit detector was a lot more sophisticated than that of the girls in the Bible study group.

christened him "Mr. Fun." I felt real tears running down my cheeks.

Dr. Turner looked satisfied. "I can see you understand what I mean. Sometimes therapists forget to look at the whole picture. He's told you your glass is half empty. Maybe it's half full. No parents are perfect, Cassandra. But most of us struggle to do our best. You may need to look for the silver lining."

"I was about ready to come in there after you," said Laura, when I located her in the tropical fish department of the pet store at the end of the strip mall. "You look like hell. Let's go get a drink and some real food. I got a recommendation for a French place in Venice. My treat—it's a good-luck splurge." I was happy to turn the reins over to her.

Over a crabmeat imperial crêpe, spinach soufflé, and a glass of Chardonnay, I updated Laura on the events surrounding Kaitlin's lawsuit and Bencher's murder, including my visits to the Bible study group and Dr. Turner.

"Jeanine said that Turner's organization has been very active lately. She says he's ruthless."

Laura rolled her eyes. "Mind if I ask a few questions here?" I knew she'd ask them even if I did mind.

"What was in the folders you saw on Bencher's floor?"

"I don't know. I didn't have the time or the wherewithal to read them," I said.

"Okay. What was on the floor around the folders?"

"Nothing important, as far as I could tell. Shards of glass from the broken coffeepot."

"Did you see or hear anyone in the office or out in the hallway after you found Bencher?"

"No."

Chapter 13

Finally it was here: my first day of School, with a knee-knocking capital *S*. When I pulled into the club in the near darkness at 6:30, the range was deserted. Now, with the first streaks of sun lighting up the golf course like a carpet of emeralds, every centimeter of the practice area was filled. And no lighthearted chitchat today. I heard only the crack of balls whistling out into the range and the quiet murmur of caddies coaching their golfers. Laura had roared off on a quick tour of our first hurdle—the Bobcat course—with my notes and the LPGA yardage book in hand.

As Mike's caddie on the PGA Tour, I'd loved this moment in a golf tournament most of all. Not one shot had been officially struck, so in theory, anything was possible. There was no discouraging high round from yesterday to overcome, no muffed shot from the last hole to forget, not even a fantastic finish to live up to. None of the confidence-crushing history of previous rounds. There

look good if they made it onto the Tour using his equipment. Girls who'd make any clubs look good, anywhere.

"Cassie, how are you?" I stopped my pacing, astonished to see Max Harding in front of me.

"What the hell are you doing here?"

"Here at the tournament? Business. Here with you? I've been wanting to talk to you since I ran into you the other night at Chili-Dippers."

"This is a lousy time to talk. I'm teeing off in forty-five minutes."

He nodded. "I know. Sorry. Maybe I can catch up with you later. Hey, good luck. I know you're going to be great." I watched him walk all the way back to the clubhouse. He filled out the yellow Cutter and Buck golf shirt just as well as he had the business suit I saw him in last week. I returned to the putting green for one last session.

"Putter and I are one," I muttered. I jabbed at a practice Titleist ball. It went screaming past the hole I was shooting for.

"Let's go," said Laura. "Ten minutes to blastoff."

We met our playing partners waiting on the path leading up to the first tee. I introduced Laura to Julie Atwater. I wasn't sure whether it would help or hinder to share a cart and play with her again today, not that I had any say about it. On the bright side, she'd be familiar, and familiar was good. On the dark side, we'd both played lousy yesterday—just seeing her here brought that springing clearly to mind. I knew we'd stay away from discussions about her possibly confused sexuality or my problems with finding dead bodies. That could only help my focus.

Our third contestant, Heather Boyle, had brought her fiancé as caddie and her mother as gallery. The mother was elfin-sized, with painted eyebrows and lids, spiked hair, and pixie sparkles on her cheeks. The boyfriend looked more like a banker than a caddie—blond and solid,

"Say a prayer that it goes straight," whispered Heather's mother. Heather swung, producing a low, straight ball that skimmed the center of the fairway and rolled up the hill and out of sight.

"Nice ball," said Julie, taking her place on the tee. Her drive leaned right and skidded into the fairway bunker she'd found the day before.

"Next on the tee, Cassandra Burdette from Myrtle Beach, South Carolina." My legs felt wobbly and my arms like overcooked Ramen noodles. Laura smiled reassurance. The other girls were smiling, too. More, I assumed, from the relief of getting off the tee themselves than for my benefit.

I waggled my three-wood and stared down the fairway. "You can do it," I whispered. "Let it go." I coiled up and launched an adrenaline-powered drive that landed just short of where Heather's ball had come to rest.

"Good start," said Laura, as I hopped into the cart and roared by with Julie. When we reached my ball, I chose a seven-iron without hesitation and hit it to the back of the green. A triumph—a birdie try on the first hole. Never mind that the putt was unsinkable by anyone outside of Tiger Woods. I leaned over against the cart to stretch my calf muscles while the others hit their second shots.

"Do you have something going with that Gary?" Laura asked, breathing hard from her jog up the fairway.

The blood rushing to my face felt hot. "What do you mean?"

"You know what I mean," she said. "The little public massage. The 'she's got a bright future' routine. Does that guy have the hots for you?"

"That's Kaitlin's brother," I said, not addressing her question. "I know him from high school and we've talked some about the tournament and the mess she's in."

"We've got the time," said her fiancé. Easy for him to be cheerful: Heather had shown no flaws in her game so far.

"What's Max Harding doing down here?" asked Laura as we waited.

"He said business."

"He's Coach Rupert's lawyer now?" I nodded. "Why would that bring him here?" I shrugged.

"These girls are so slow our clothes will be out of style by the time we finish the round," said Heather.

"Don't sweat the small stuff," said her fiancé. I wondered if they'd spend a lifetime of marriage speaking in clichés.

By the time the girls ahead finally cleared the green, I felt even tighter than I had on the first tee. I popped my drive up short of the green.

"At least it's not wet," said Laura. "And chipping's your game."

Was my game, I thought, after chunking the shot fifteen yards short of the flag. I banged my ball up the hill. Instead of curving gently to the left and dropping into the cup as I'd predicted, the putt held its line and hung out six inches from the hole.

"Tough break," said Laura. "You made a good run at it."

I stomped off to the fourth tee. Heather teed off with another screaming drive and Julie followed closely on her heels.

I could feel the gears churning in my brain. There are two kinds of golfers out there, those who play by understanding mechanics and those who play by feel. The mechanical players, like Nick Faldo, are always tinkering with their swing. They want to know precisely where the toe of the club should point at each position on the backswing. They've spent hours with slow-motion vide-

"Say a prayer that it goes in," said Heather's mother as her daughter stood over her putt. God was going to be awfully busy this afternoon, watching over each of Heather's shots. She sank the birdie putt and walked off the green into her fiancé's embrace.

I, without the benevolent intervention of either a mother or a higher power, pulled my birdie putt left. "Shit!" I said, not so softly. "We might as well be playing putt-putt golf in a trailer park. There's no way I can concentrate with that racket going on."

Laura nodded. "Let me know if I can help," she said.

"You can muzzle that freaking mutt," I said. "Now that would be helpful."

We made the turn with me four over par, not a good omen even by Laura's ever-optimistic standards.

"The hell with a training regimen," I said. "I need a big, fat hot dog, maybe two. Mustard, sauerkraut, and onions. And if they sold Budweiser, I'd buy one of those too."

"What training regimen?" Laura laughed. We ordered hot dogs and chips and stuffed them down while we waited for the tenth tee to clear.

par five, but at least I'd managed to scrape along without any penalty shots. Overall, holding steady. Then, an enormous crack of thunder clapped overhead, followed by one prolonged horn blast coming from the direction of the distant clubhouse.

"That's the warning siren! We've got to take shelter," said Heather's fiancé. "They said not to hit another shot after play is suspended." We all piled on the golf carts and rode to the shelter attached to the rest room to wait out the storm. Heather and her entourage began to discuss the merits of her new putting stroke.

"What's your beef with Gary Rupert?" I asked Julie, preferring to make conversation about anything other than golf.

"He's arrogant," she said. "He hit on me last month. Since I turned him down, he acts like we've never spoken. I hate that kind of guy—everything, including common decency, revolves around whether you worship their sex appeal."

I didn't say anything. Truth was, Gary had been nothing but charming as far as I was concerned. I could empathize with the "hit on" experience, but from my perspective, it was rather exciting.

Two more cartloads of golfers and their caddies streamed into the shelter, drenched from the sudden downpour. A tall woman with a long, narrow face and very dark eyebrows was shrieking at her caddie. "Damn it to hell, I know the goddamn rules. I played on the damn Tour for two years. Do you think I'd risk my damn career doing something that stupid?"

"I think she was trying to be helpful," the caddie offered.

"Calling in the rules official to chastise us? You call that helpful?" The tall woman poked a finger in her caddie's chest. "I'm warning you," she said. "Keep that bitch

"She needs kindness, too," said Julie, her voice quiet. "Jesus didn't only befriend people who were easy to get along with."

The hour we spent waiting out the thunderstorm improved no one's game, including mine. Even Heather, with heaven and her mother watching over her, hit her tee shot out of bounds on fourteen and took a double bogey. I had managed a birdie on the par-three fifteenth, but lost that advantage with three-putts for bogeys on the final two holes. A big, fat seventy-seven: five strokes over par for the course and nowhere close to the score of my dreams.

"Not that I had that much to work with after the front nine," I said to Laura as we walked off the eighteenth green. "What's a couple more three-putts if you're not going to make the cut anyway."

"That's a lousy attitude," said Laura. I checked over and countersigned my card, then turned it in to the scorer's tent. Kaitlin and Gary were arriving from the ninth hole as we left. Out of Kaitlin's line of sight, Gary saluted me with a smile and a thumbs-up.

"I heard you shot the second lowest score today, Miss Rupert," a bystander said. "I'm with Golfnews Online. Could I have a few words with you when you finish here?"

"Let's hang around a minute," said Laura. "I want to hear this."

"How was it out there?" the reporter asked when Kaitlin emerged from the tent.

"I had a fantastic day," she said. "I played great. I hit greens; my putter was hot so I made some birdies. It was more fun than I could have imagined."

"There had to be a lot of pressure out on the course today. How did you keep your focus?"

"I just hit every shot as though this was my last day ever playing golf," said Kaitlin. "That way, everything

"He's not altogether wrong about that," I whispered to Laura.

"I can't even believe he's related to Julie," she whispered back. "She seems so normal."

We made a wide circle around Julie's father and approached the scoreboard that dominated the west side of the clubhouse. The scores from the morning had already been posted. The low round, sixty-seven, belonged to So Won Lee.

"Now there's a score you could sleep like a baby on," I said to Laura.

"Haven't you ever heard the expression 'sleeping on the lead'?" she asked. "It's a different kind of pressure, but pressure all the same. Most players I've seen shoot a super-low score like that blew up in the next round."

Kaitlin and Gary Rupert watched as her name was inscribed in Black Magic marker under the number sixty-eight, just below So Won Lee's sixty-seven. She accepted the congratulations of a cluster of players, then swept off toward the locker room. With the help of Laura's not so gentle persuasion, I dragged myself back to the putting green. There were demons to slay—I had to put today behind me, taking from it only what I could use profitably in tomorrow's round.

"I'm thinking about changing my grip back over to the right hand down," I told Laura.

"I don't think you need to change anything," she said. "Your stroke looks terrific. Let's just work on tempo." We putted for half an hour—first, long lag putts, then dozens of short no-brainers that could turn into knee-knockers under the high-beam pressure of the tournament.

"I need a break," I said. We stretched out on a bench in the shade. "You were going to tell me your theory about me and men."

chance to see you much. I'll be fine. I'm just going to get to bed early and rest up for tomorrow."

"Sure you don't mind?"

I nodded vigorously. As she concluded her conversation with her aunt, loud voices drifted over from the driving range. I turned and saw Kaitlin screaming at Walter Moore.

"I thought we had an exclusive deal here," she said. Her complexion had flushed to a mottled red and a hank of hair had sprung loose from her usually perfect ponytail.

"I said we would sponsor you. I never said you would be the only one that we sponsored."

"She's Oriental, for God's sake," said Kaitlin. "You think that's going to sell golf clubs?" Now her voice verged on hysterical.

"She hits the ball longer than any woman I've ever seen. You included. That's what sells golf clubs," said Walter. "And just for your information, Oriental is for rugs. Asian is for people." He stalked away, leaving her fuming alone on the range.

"Tut, tut," murmured Laura. "A lovers' spat."

"Go, Walter," I said. "I wouldn't have believed he had that much backbone in him."

"Afternoon, ladies," said the gravelly voice of Sheriff Pate. The bench creaked as he lowered his bulk down next to Laura. He sighed and mopped his forehead with a graying handkerchief. "I thought the thunderstorm would cool things off."

"I'm Laura Snow. You must be Sheriff Pate." She shook his hand. "You guys had your hands full out there today."

"You're tellin' me," he said, puffing up at her recognition of his importance.

"Any progress on the Bencher case?"

Chapter 15

Laura left me at the Cracker Barrel, happily gorging myself on meat loaf, fried okra, and biscuits dogpaddling in sausage gravy. I didn't feel tired by the time I returned to the room, though I knew I should follow my own advice about getting to bed early. I'd hate to run out of steam halfway through tomorrow's round. I washed up and got into bed with the thriller I'd brought with me. After I'd read the first chapter three times, I gave up and turned out the light.

Against my will, my mind began to run over my performance today, lingering painfully on the bogey putts on one, two, three, five, thirteen, seventeen, and eighteen. Anyway you looked at it, seventy-seven could not be considered an LPGA-quality performance. Then my mind shifted seamlessly to the Panther course. I began to review all the ways I could get into trouble, especially on the holes comprising the Panther's Claw.

of the female population of the high school. I'd overheard girls gossiping in the hallways about why he'd chosen me—a small, gawky, shy, tomboy golfer—instead of one of the popular and glamorous cheerleaders who'd have killed to take my place. All of which meant I had a long way to fall when he dumped me without explanation. If I was willing to dig around, I could still feel the deep well of shame and hurt I'd locked away ten years ago.

But I wasn't willing, so back to the facts. What was he really doing at Q-school? It seemed unlikely that Kaitlin's lawsuit would have brought him down to Florida, unless he had business with the False Memory Consociation. It occurred to me that the guy I'd seen talking to Gary Rupert in the bar the other night looked a great deal like Max. Then I remembered my mother's phone message about Max coming into the restaurant for lunch. It made no sense that he would be in Florida on Saturday, Myrtle Beach on Sunday, then back in Florida today.

But speaking of Gary, what was up with that? If Laura was right and we had something going, I had no idea what it was. I wished Jack Wolfe were here. I knew part of the problem was just plain loneliness. In the end, having a boyfriend seven thousand miles away was about as much use as having no one at all. Besides which, Jack would know exactly how it felt to be in my position. He'd been through his own Q-school nightmare last year. And he had a way of taking things so easily.

"You're tense, Cassie. Go ahead and have a beer," I imagined him saying. In honor of Jack, and bowing to my spinning brain, I got up and cracked open the second-to-last can of Busch. Halfway through the last can, the phone rang.

"Cassie, it's Joe. I hope I'm not waking you up. How are you? How was the day?"

"At least he's a player," I said. "He's not one of those guys that stands around telling other people how to do it."

"Fine," said Joe. "But he barely earned a dime on the Tour, and as a reward, he got himself banished halfway around the world." I heard him breathe in sharply. "I'm sorry. I didn't call to fight with you. I only wanted to wish you well." His voice was very formal now.

I matched his tone. "Thank you. I'd better get some rest."

I lay back down and turned out the light. I reviewed the conversation with Joe, then caromed back to the seven three-putts, then back to Joe. Things were out of control if I was even picking fights with him—a paragon of unflappability. There was no way I would sleep now. I got up, threw on my jeans and a T-shirt, and walked to the nearby convenience store to buy more beer.

As I got off the elevator, I heard the phone ringing through the door of my room. I struggled to slide the card key into the lock, ran inside, and grabbed the phone. With all fingers and toes crossed, I hoped it would be Jack.

"Cassie? It's Max Harding. I'm sorry to call you so late." I was silent. Shocked, actually. Almost as if I'd conjured him up again, just by thinking about him. "Um, your mom gave me your phone number. I know it was bad timing to try to talk to you earlier today. I wanted to apologize to you for that. And for high school."

"For high school?" Jesus, wasn't he about ten years too late? His hoarse breathing filled the receiver.

"Gosh, this is harder than I thought it would be. I'd really like to do this in person. Could I come by for a few minutes and talk to you? I feel terrible about what's happened."

"I don't think so. Jesus, Max. Give it a rest. That was ten years ago. It's late and I'm tired. What could we possibly have to say to each other?"

"You must think I'm a real rat." He sighed. "I know it looks bad—what happened after that night on the beach."

"No," I said. "It looked pretty good for you. It looked like you were out to get laid for the night, and you did. You got just what you wanted. I was a big, dumb sucker. End of story."

"That's not it, Cass. I loved being with you. I really meant to call you. I wish I could explain it now, I wish I could have then." He tore strips off the label of the beer bottle and balled them up while I waited for him to go on.

"Remember when we cut Mr. Romero's class and drove down to Savannah?"

"Dave wanted to kill both of us," I said. "Mom thought grounding me for life would be enough punishment."

"How about the time it snowed two inches and they closed school?"

"We drove all over town trying to borrow a sled," I said, laughing. "The trash can lids worked pretty well, though."

"We had a lot of fun together," Max said. He reached over and brushed a strand of hair off my forehead.

"Why are we discussing this now?" I said, pulling back out of his range. "I won't lie to you, you really hurt my feelings. But I got along fine without you. And you and Brenda have done just dandy, too, from the sound of it." Max winced. "We made a mistake. It's medieval history now." I stood up and strode to the door. "Thanks for your concern. I think you should leave."

Max followed me across the room. "But that's what I came to say. I don't think that night was a mistake. I've thought about it every day since then. You are the most beautiful woman I've ever known. You're strong." He squeezed my bicep. "And soft at the same time." His fingers barely touched my cheek.

much as I wish it were different, I guess I should never have come."

I straightened my clothes, confused and drunk. "Just get the fuck out, Max." I had no pity for the agony in his face.

"I'm really sorry if I hurt you. I'm more sorry that what should have been a beginning had to end."

"Nice closing statement, Counselor." I walked to the door and jerked it open. "You didn't even bother with the fucking Boone's Farm Apple Wine this time."

"I'm sorry. I'm sorry." He stumbled slightly and caught himself on the doorjamb. "Good luck tomorrow. Take care."

I slammed the door closed behind him.

I won't think about this, I said to myself, my body rigid with anger and shame. It's best to go on as if this hadn't happened. I hooked my bra closed, tugged tight the corners of the bedspread, straightened the faded drapes, hurled Max's beer bottle into the trash. Three-pointer. I took a hundred practice swings in the mirror with the Ben Hogan nine-iron. Then I lay awake on the bed until almost four, searching for a way to block out my feelings.

Drapes: vertical. TV: horizontal. Highboy: vertical. Hide-a-Bed: horizontal.

But the lingering humiliation was strong—too powerful even for Joe Lancaster's mental techniques. Six A.M. could not come soon enough.

"Looked like she was hot at you yesterday."

"She understands that I have to run a business," Walter said. "She knows that what we have going between us means a whole lot more than a Deikon logo on somebody's bag."

I wasn't altogether certain he was right on that one, but I wasn't going to argue with him either.

"You're not eating much this morning," he said. I looked down at my tray. I'd forced down a few bites of Raisin Bran and half a stale blueberry muffin. Last night's overload of beer still bloated my system.

"Nerves," I said. "I'll get something later. See you over at the club."

"You look tired," said Laura when I arrived at the range. "Sleep okay?"

"Fine." No way was I going to tell her about the visit from Max. Bad enough that it happened, that I'd allowed things to go as far as they had. How could I explain that I'd let a guy who hadn't touched me or even talked to me in over ten years practically strip me half naked? And worse yet, that I might very well have slept with him, if his *wife* hadn't beeped him from home? So far, the cost of surviving the Q-school pressure cooker seemed to be the erosion of my better judgment.

Perhaps I'd sort out the events of last night later under Dr. Baxter's careful tutelage. Or maybe I'd never bring them up at all—bury them deep in my memory's back boneyard. In any event, I was determined that none of this would interfere with my golf round today.

"Walter likes a winner, doesn't he?" said Laura. She pointed down the range, where he stood talking to So Won Lee. He had one of her clubs in his hand. I imagined he was describing all of its many shortcomings.

"You don't need to go for medalist," he said, winking back in our direction. "Play smart." She split the fairway with a long, screaming drive.

"Thank God," said her mother.

"That's a beauty! And you met your first goal," said the fiancé. "Hit the fairway on one."

Neither her tee shot nor her marital status have any bearing on your performance, I told myself.

Julie and I teed off in quick succession, her ball curving into the right rough, mine heading left. All three of us made par by hitting the green in regulation, followed by two putts.

"There's your second goal, par on the first," said the fiancé, as Heather plucked her ball from the cup. Julie and I rode in silence to the second tee.

I knew the best strategy today was to block the cut out of my mind. Heather's fiancé had it right. I could only play one shot at a time, and none of them would be executed well if I was thinking about the whole round, the whole tournament, or my whole life. I envied the woman who watched us from the screened-in porch around her pool as we climbed the stairs to the second tee. From where I stood, she had no stress at all.

We began to get a good idea of how fast the greens were on the second hole. Julie and Heather's drives both skidded across the green, passing the hole on their way. I dubbed my tee shot short, then chipped my ball by the hole along the same line I'd seen the others take. Two putts later, I carded my first bogey of the day.

We followed a long stretch of cart path and turned the corner into the third hole. The early morning sun hit the heavy dew on the fairway, making the grass almost indistinguishable from the lake that lined the left side.

"I'll be glad to be finished with this course," said Heather, after blasting another drive dead center down the fairway.

"It's not worth it," she said. "Just take your lumps and move on. We'll make a birdie later."

"No, it's worth a shot," I said. "I've got all the room I need."

"You're pressing too hard," she said.

"I'll be fine. I'll get my eight up fast and over."

She backed off. I swung hard. The ball soared up, nicked the last frond of the palm tree directly in line with the green, and plopped back down just twenty feet ahead of us. This time, without any further consultation, I chipped out into the open fairway, hit a wedge on, and two-putted for triple bogey.

"You'll never have to see that hole again," said Laura.

Now I felt a fierce concentration settle over me. I swore I would not make another dim-witted, bone-headed error. I was not exactly in what sportswriters call the zone, but it was a different territory compared to my jittery start. Nothing distracted me from my focus—not the endearments of Heather's fiancé, not the escalating prayers of Heather's mother, not Julie's rapidly disintegrating performance. She double-bogeyed three of the four holes of the Panther's Claw. I parred all of them, then birdied the par five sixteenth.

"Almost there, girls," said Heather's fiancé.

"It's all in God's hands anyway," said Heather's mother. "God has a plan for each of us." I thought she glanced at me and Julie with pity. As though her Heather was all set, but only God knew what our particular plans might be. Heather and I each drove safely into the fairway on seventeen. Julie pulled her shot just far enough left to catch the out-of-bounds stake marking the outside edge of the driving range.

"That's just the kind of day it's been." She sighed and teed up a second ball, which again rolled over the staked OB line and then dropped off into the pit containing the

"It wasn't your day."

We rode over to the clubhouse in silence and watched the volunteers record our scores. Eve and Mary, whom I'd eaten dinner with at Chili's Saturday night, arrived shortly after us. Eve's total, 145, looked to be safely inside the cut. Mary's 160 looked clearly out. The Bible study leaders, Nicki and Joanne, stood to one side, waiting for their scores to be posted.

I began to understand at a gut-twisting level how hard competition was among friends. I wanted these girls to do well—I knew how much it meant to each of them. But sitting on the bubble of the cut, I knew their performances were not independent of mine. Only the low seventy scores and ties would go on to play tomorrow. Go on to try to live the dream. This exhilarating, crazy dream we all shared.

"Let's get out of here," said Laura. "We won't know anything about the cut until the afternoon threesomes come in. We can't stand around here all day. We'll lose what little is left of our minds. Let's get some lunch. Maybe we can even catch forty winks."

mind to even try Q-school. If I just missed at 152, I'd be haunted by one shot, any shot, that could have moved me into the second half of the tournament. Maybe the stupid heroics I tried on the eighth hole today. Or any of the three-putts I'd muddled through yesterday. With the cut at 151, I could choose two shots to beat myself up over. The combinations would be unlimited.

An unsmiling official approached the scoreboard with an enormous pair of cardboard scissors. She held them up in the space directly above my name with one hand and extracted a roll of Scotch tape from her pocket with the other. Just then, I heard a commotion coming from the direction of the LPGA office.

"Hold off on that," called out Alice MacPherson as she hurried toward the crowd. "We need to make an adjustment. There's been a disqualification." The golfers around me broke out into excited chatter.

Alice smoothed the piece of paper in her hand and cleared her throat. "Ms. So Won Lee of Korea has been disqualified from the LPGA Sectional Qualifying Tournament for the use of illegal equipment—a nonconforming driving club."

The buzz from the crowd escalated, almost obscuring one high, piercing scream that had to belong to the Korean player. The scoring official peered at the paper Alice held out, then marched over to So Won's name. She wrote across it in large red Magic Marker letters: DQ. After consulting with the other officials, she picked up the cardboard scissors and taped them just below my name.

"I'll be damned," said Laura. "You made it!" She hugged me hard. "You made it, you crazy woman. We did it!" She began to perform a war dance around me.

"Excuse me, may I have your attention for another moment, ladies," said Alice MacPherson. "Members of the press are located in a tent next to the practice putting

a stunt like this? You and me—we are finished. Washed up, sweetheart."

Kaitlin unfastened his hands from her arms and stepped back out of his reach. "First of all," she said in an ice cold voice, "I didn't do anything. I had nothing to do with putting that stinking club in that bitch's bag. Second"— she brushed off her shirt where his hands had gripped her shoulders. "Second, you big, dumb oaf. We certainly are finished because we never were started. I can't believe you were stupid enough to think for one minute that I was interested in anything but your equipment. No, let me re-phrase that to make it quite clear—not your equipment, your *golf* clubs. Now get away from me before I call security." She gave him the same quick shove she'd given her mother that first morning back in South Carolina. Only Walter, significantly larger and more solid than Kait-lin's mother, did not lose his balance.

I had never seen anyone look as angry as Walter Moore. The twitches that I'd noticed during our two breakfasts now resulted in bulging eyes and fierce jerking movements in his lips and cheeks.

"His birdie is cooked," I said to Laura. "He's lost two endorsement deals—So Won's out of the tournament, and Kaitlin's a nightmare. Plus, you know he's got to be in hot water over the discovery of the illegal club. He nearly had heart failure when I asked him about it. He wasn't supposed to have shown it to anyone yet. He was just grandstanding for Kaitlin's benefit."

"Do you think she really put it in So Won's bag?" said Laura. "Why would it mean that much to her to be in first place, halfway through the tournament? I could under-stand it a little better if all the rounds were over."

"I don't understand the girl, myself," I said. "Maybe she didn't believe she could ever beat So Won fair and square." I felt the vibration of my cell phone in my back

"I'll be fine," I said. "Go. Take the car. I can catch a ride over to the motel. I'll work a couple hours here, eat a good dinner, and turn in early. We don't tee off tomorrow until later in the morning anyway."

I worked at the practice range until dusk, mostly sticking to the plan Laura and I had agreed on. No last-minute grip shifts, no new swing thoughts, just a couple hours of smooth tempo and visualization of success on the course. Ha. Okay, so there were a few negative thoughts regarding the fact that every iron I had hit today leaked right. And how the hell could I have skulled two chips when I hadn't produced a line-drive trajectory that plug-ugly since the eighth grade? Not to mention the small matter of one-third of my attempts on the short grass resulting in three-putts. I tried to push away the doubts that whispered I didn't belong in the contest tomorrow. I'd show myself and everyone else that my place here had been earned and was deserved.

One of the volunteers flagged me down on the putting green. I wasn't in the mood to talk. A pounding headache and my fragile grip on an optimistic outlook for round three took the urge for chit-chat with a stranger right out of me.

"Cassie," she said. "Aren't you Cassie Burdette? Did you hear that Kaitlin missed her interview this evening?" She had the breathless voice of someone who couldn't wait to tell you their news, because the more people she told and the more personal details she had to tell, the more important she felt. "They looked for her everywhere. Do you have any idea what happened to her?"

"I have no clue," I said. "We're not friends."

The volunteer scurried off, I assumed in search of someone who'd turn out to be a more sympathetic listener and less of a grump. I ambled over in the direction of the clubhouse to look for a ride home to the Starlight. The

Chapter 18

As dusk fell, I walked to Kaitlin's condo by way of the Bobcat's eighteenth fairway. Earlier today, I'd assumed I would never see this hole again. Now I had two more shots at it. I cut through a hedge and found the Ruperts' entranceway. Inside the vestibule, the door to their apartment was just cracked open. My knock echoed in the tiled hallway.

"Kaitlin," I called. "Hello. Gary. It's Cassie. Kaitlin! Anybody home?"

No answer. I knocked and called three more times.

The Ruperts' neighbor stuck his head out from his door. "Time to take a hike, girlie. Either they aren't home or they don't want company. Whichever it is, scram." He slammed his door shut.

Now, a dilemma. The last time I stepped uninvited through someone's open doorway, I'd discovered a dying, soon to be dead, man. One of those in a lifetime was enough. On the other hand, if either of the Ruperts was

her parents arriving at Q-school, given the bad blood between them. And how she could possibly manage to make
things "nicey-nice" with Walter Moore, given the lather
he'd worked himself into this afternoon.

I walked back to the clubhouse to look for a ride home.
The only light shone from a room near the dining hall,
which had been turned into a temporary first aid station
for the Q-school contestants.

"Can I help you?" asked the young man seated at the
desk just inside the room. He smiled and gestured to the
book he'd been reading. "Anatomy," he told me without
my asking. "I'm starting medical school in the fall and I
want to have a head start before I get there. They say it's
brutal the first year."

"Sorry to bother you, then," I said. "I was hoping to
catch a ride back to my motel."

The student ran his fingers through his blond brush cut.
"As far as I know, everyone's gone home for the day. It
was a happenin' scene here, I suppose you heard. Everyone was bushed. Would you like me to call you a taxi?"

I nodded. This guy might not know anything about
medicine yet, but at least he had the makings of a good
bedside manner. I hoped his years in med school wouldn't
wipe that out. He dialed and spoke to the dispatcher at
Triple-A Taxi.

"All the cabs are out at the moment, but they'll send
someone over ASAP. It might be half an hour," he told
me after he'd hung up.

"Damn," I said. Then belatedly, "Thanks." I felt too
antsy to just sit and wait. "I guess I'll go over to the range
and pace off some distances. The accuracy of my irons
wasn't all that great today." Not that he cared about my
golf game. "Could you send the taxi over if they show up
before I get back?" The student nodded and returned to
his anatomy text.

The medical student and I approached the pit. He held out a small penlight attached to his key ring. I flashed it over the bottom of the hole. A woman's body lay crumpled in one corner. In spite of the dim light, I was quite sure it was Kaitlin Rupert. I directed myself to observe the scene clinically, as Sheriff Pate, or even Joe Lancaster, would have done. I would not give into either the wave of nausea that flooded me or the powerful urge to scream and run.

A skimpy white lace brassiere and underpants had been stripped from Kaitlin's body and lay tangled on the loose dirt beside her. Along with her white-gold hair, they were saturated with blood. A golf club appeared to be embedded in the side of her head. The medical student nudged me aside and peered into the pit. There was a moment of stunned silence.

"I haven't finished reading the chapter on the brain," said the student. "But I'd say it's a nine-iron to the parietal lobe."

"It's not a nine-iron," I said. My voice came out tight and shrill. "It's a driver. It looks a lot like the Fairway Bruiser. Titanium shaft and illegally inflated coefficient of restitution, creating a springlike effect in the club face. Or on someone's brain. Outlawed according to Appendix II, 5a, the USGA Rules of Golf." And Kaitlin said I didn't know the rules.

"Are you feeling all right?" the student asked. He grabbed my forearm, guided me back from the edge of the excavation, and began to grope for my pulse. "Put your head between your knees if you feel faint. It's not uncommon for the layperson to feel woozy when they encounter the scene of an accident."

"This was no accident," I said.

The student keeled over and did a face plant into the grass.

my feelings about discovering Kaitlin suddenly gave way. I sank to a squat beside the cruiser and began to cry.

"Get back in the vehicle," said Pate. "We're going to take a ride to the station."

At the sheriff's department, my interrogation did not wind down until after ten o'clock. I reviewed my movements during the entire evening for two different officers. Their questions took two unpleasant turns. First, the following irrefutable fact was established: I had found not one, but two, dead bodies in the short span of two weeks. No one knew this more vividly than I did.

Second, I had benefited from So Won Lee's elimination out of the golf tournament. Because of the illegal golf club found in her bag, I had squeaked into the second half of the tournament. Making me a logical perpetrator for the misplaced club. And now that same golf club had turned up as an apparent murder weapon. Were these events connected? I had no clue. I had no reasonable explanation for either of them. I reported in detail my conversations over the last week and a half with Walter Moore and Kaitlin herself, hoping they might shift suspicion from me to someone else. At this point, anyone would do.

"Sheriff Pate," I began.

"Sheriff Pate?" hooted one of the other officers. "In his dreams, he's Sheriff Pate. Low-down-on-the-totem-pole Deputy Pate, to you." Pate squirmed with discomfort as several of the deputies taunted him.

Why the hell had he lied to me about his title?

"We are not intending to arrest you tonight, Miss Burdette," said the only deputy who had not participated in razzing Pate. "But you may not leave this county until we inform you that you may go. Is that clear enough?"

I nodded. This implied threat made Detective Maloney's desire to keep in touch after I'd found Bencher's body feel positively chummy. Evidently, the police had

plans to teach Kaitlin Rupert a lesson. Now that she's turned up dead, that plan is going to look really bad for him."

"How does he know she's dead? They only found her a couple of hours ago."

"I have no idea. You told me to call if I heard something. I'm just keeping my word. If you wanted to look at any of his papers, it's now or never."

"I'm glad you called. Let me think a minute, it's been a crazy night." I was not in any mood to snoop around someone's office. I was in deep shit with the authorities already. On the other hand, my father always said, if you're in a hole and someone hands you a shovel, shut up and start digging.

"First problem," I said. "I'm at the sheriff's department and I don't have a car."

"No problem there. I live right around the corner," she said. "I'll pick you up in a few." She didn't give me time to elaborate on problems two, three, four, and five, all related to reasons why I ought to just go home and mind my own business.

"What kind of questions?"

"Just stuff about what I'd noticed when you were here. What we talked about."

"You didn't tell him I was pretending to be a patient?"

"Of course not!" Jeanine frowned. "I was so excited about the golf, I did tell him about your being here for the tournament and how you were going to help me meet Rick. Was that all right?" It didn't feel all right, but she looked too upset to scold.

"Let's take a quick look around," I said. "And then get the hell out of here. What exactly do you think we'll find?"

"I'm not certain myself. But he was talking about the Rupert suit. I heard him tell some guy on the phone that they needed to clear everything out of the office tonight. They're supposed to meet here after midnight." She looked at her watch. "That gives us almost two hours."

"Does he make hard copies of all his documents, or should we start with the computer?"

"Gosh, the girl who comes in on Fridays is forever filing, so I know there are records in those cabinets." She waved at the row of green metal file cabinets against the far wall. "Rupert starts with *R*. I'd start there, if I were you. Turner's a logical kind of guy. In some ways, anyway."

"Great. Why don't you keep an eye out for trouble?"

Jeanine moved to the front room and peered through the dusty slats of the Venetian blinds in the waiting area. I began to flip through the files in the top drawer of the third cabinet. Halfway toward the back of the drawer, I found "Rupert, Kaitlin/Peter." It was a thick folder, stuffed so full I could hardly pull it out, even using two hands.

"There's someone pulling into the parking lot!" Jeanine's voice shook.

Rupert girl dead, the cops are probably gearing up to search the place. I can't risk leaving this stuff here."

"Somebody tipped them off?"

"Christ, Vinnie. Everyone's gonna know we backed her father financially. It won't take a genius to make the connection. Besides, there was a girl here Monday snooping around, asking questions about the organization," said Turner.

"So who killed Rupert?"

"How the hell would I know?" said Turner.

"Could it have been Atwater? I told you that guy was nuts. All those damn crazy Bible verses. I told you not to get involved with him. . . ."

"You're a fucking genius, looking backward. We all are. Shut up and get to work."

"We need empty boxes," said Turner's companion. "We can't carry all this out loose."

Jeanine clutched my hand. She must have had the same thought I did: the logical—the only—place to look for boxes was in our closet. And from the general tone of their conversation, I could guess they wouldn't take discovering us in here with grace.

"I brought a couple in my trunk," Turner said. "Take the keys and I'll start pulling things out." I let out a long, slow breath.

"So lay it out for me, Will," said the second man when he returned. "What's your plan?"

"One, we need to move this stuff out. And two, shut that nosy girl up. The second job is yours."

"You think someone sent her? You think she saw something while she was here? Why the hell did you let her in?"

"Shut up, for Christ's sake. I'm not playing twenty questions. Do your job and it won't matter what she saw or why she came. With both Rupert and Bencher dead,

our closet. I heard him opening and closing drawers and rustling through their contents. "Look at the shit she keeps in here. It's like a goddamned beauty spa. Half the time, we can't even use the copier because the paper's locked away and she's forgotten where the goddamned keys are. She'd lose her own tits if they weren't right under her nose."

"Look, Will," said the second man in a conciliatory voice, "the place is empty: your nerves are getting the better of you. There's no one here but me and you. I'm going to do what I can to take care of the situation. I've been along for the ride every step of the way. But don't ask me to hurt someone. I can't do that."

"No blood, pal. Just scare the hell out of her. We're in this together, buddy, like it or not. Let's get out of here."

"One more thing," said the second man. "Do you think Jeanine would go out with me?"

"You're joking." Turner's voice was incredulous. "That girl is an intellectual zero."

"She has other charms." The man laughed. "Two of them, to be exact." Their footsteps faded into the distance. We heard them leave the front office and lock the door behind them. Jeanine let out a deep breath.

"Can we get out of here? I like you and all that, but these are tight quarters."

I flung the door open. "You were brilliant, turning the lock at just the right minute. I had no idea how we were going to explain ourselves."

"Just sheer reflex," she said, following me out into the dim shadows of the office.

"That guy's a pig. How long have you worked for him?"

"He's a horse's behind, all right, but he isn't around that much," laughed Jeanine, giddy with relief. "And for the money I make, I let his idiotic comments wash right

"Laura said you were going to bed early. I figured we wouldn't see each other until tomorrow."

I ignored his accusatory tone and ran my hand down the length of the blue sling that held Joe's left arm. "Are you okay?"

He nodded. "Where have you been?"

"It's a long story," I said. "Unbelievably long. First of all, Kaitlin's been murdered."

"*Kaitlin's* dead? No way! What happened?"

"I don't know what happened. Naturally, I found the body and the cops think I killed her." I explained about finding the corpse in the pit, lying next to what I believed was the illegal driver that had resulted in the elimination of So Won Lee. For a moment, I wrestled with whether I should confess about my break-in to Dr. Turner's office. It was late, I was beyond exhausted, and I knew Laura and Joe would want every detail. And then they'd pepper my narrative with horrified reprimands.

"There's more, isn't there?" said Laura. "You've got a very strange look on your face. A guilty one."

I sighed. "I just came from Dr. Turner's office with Jeanine. We listened to him spend the evening clearing files out that he doesn't want the police to see."

"Who's Jeanine?" asked Laura.

"Dr. Will Turner? Of the False Memory Consociation?" asked Joe at the same time. "What do you mean you *listened* to him?"

I sighed again. I explained to Joe how I'd masqueraded as a patient yesterday. Then I described tonight's adventure—Jeanine's call and our eavesdropping on Dr. Turner from the closet inside his office. "He's working with some other guy, a lawyer. He wants this guy to scare me off the trail."

"What trail?" said Laura. "I don't get what Turner has to do with any of this."

bed and pulled the spread up over my face.

"Look," said Laura. "There are a million other possible suspects. So Won Lee had an obvious motive to club Kaitlin to death. Walter Moore did, too."

"I saw him at the sheriff's department, waiting to be questioned," I said from under the bedcovers. "According to the note I saw in the Ruperts' condo, Walter was out to dinner with Kaitlin right before she died. Then there's that Leviticus guy. He was in the immediate vicinity of both the murders. And he fits into your category of a not-too-smart, but loose, cannon. Turner and his buddy mentioned his name tonight. They're worried about him, anyway, whether the cops are or not."

"Didn't Pate tell you yesterday that one of Bencher's patients already confessed to killing him?" asked Laura. "In that case, the two murders aren't even connected."

"Time out, ladies," said Joe, pulling the bedspread off my face. "Can we all agree that you need to focus on tomorrow's tournament?" Laura and I both nodded. "As I see it, ruminating about who killed Kaitlin is not congruent with that goal. So here's the plan. Close your eyes, both of you." I shut my eyes. "Now picture carrying a heavy load, something so heavy you can hardly stand up holding it." I imagined my arms full of a large package. My thighs and forearms ached from the effort of carrying it. "Now you see me come into the picture," said Joe. "My arm is fine. I look strong and solid."

"What are you wearing?" asked Laura. "Are you naked?"

"Jeans and a golf shirt, O you of the dirty mind," he said. "Now picture me taking the burden from you." I visualized handing over my heavy package. "You feel light. You feel relieved," said Joe. "Open your eyes now. In that load were all those questions about the two murders. That worry is mine now. Your only concern is your golf game. Agreed?"

Chapter 20

In spite of the late hour we'd finally gotten to sleep, I woke up at 5:30 A.M., muscle fibers twitching and brain cells spinning. Maybe a vigorous run would settle me down. I'd learned by painful experience in the first round that it didn't pay to arrive at the golf course too early. I got up and pulled on my running clothes in the dark.

"Where the hell are you going?" asked Laura, her voice muffled by two pillows.

"Out for a jog. I'm too anxious to just sit around."

"You'll stay around the motel, then?" said Laura. "I don't want anything happening to you on my watch. Doc said you weren't to go out alone."

"So come along."

"Gimme a break. Not a chance I'm going jogging in the pitch dark. Can't you use the gym downstairs?"

"Their equipment is pathetic," I said. "And I'll lose my mind if I wait around here until tee time." I knew Laura and Joe both meant well, but the weight of their good-

exercise. I knew Laura could be talked into my favorite breakfast at the Cracker Barrel—cheddar cheese omelet with ham, sausage, *and* bacon, plus sausage gravy and biscuits on the side. A truckload of heart-stopping sludge, yes, but just what the golf doctor would prescribe to help cushion the collapse of a long-time dream.

As I pulled into the parking lot at the club, my headlights flashed over a hunched figure hurrying toward the clubhouse. I stomped on the brakes and lurched to a stop next to Alice MacPherson. She appeared distracted, unaware that my rented Pontiac had nearly flattened her.

I rolled down the window. "It's awful news about Kaitlin Rupert." Wouldn't pay to appear only interested in my own concerns.

Alice nodded. "Unbelievable." She continued walking briskly toward the clubhouse.

"Is everything still on here?"

She nodded again, calling back over her shoulder, "No changes. Lucky for us, the crime scene is contained to the other golf course so we'll be able to proceed as planned on the Bobcat. I'm telling all the girls, you'll need to make yourself available to the sheriff's department for questioning, as they request. Oh, and we will be holding a memorial service for Kaitlin after the afternoon round. I'm estimating sometime around four, depending on the weather this afternoon. And speed of play." Just mentioning the possibility of slow play brought a scowl to her face. She rushed off in the direction of the anxious-looking group of volunteers huddled at the entrance to her office.

I locked the car, crossed the road, and started off at a fast clip down the Panther's first fairway. Laura would kill me when I got back. But the conversation with Alice left me feeling like I needed to see the site where I'd found Kaitlin's body. This time in the daylight.

Really, there was nothing in those words that I couldn't have thought of myself. That I hadn't already told myself, for that matter. But Joe had a way about him, as soothing as a cat's purr, a well-worn baby's blanket, warm milk.

You're losing it, Cassie, I told myself.

I picked up the pace until I was breathing hard and hoarse. I passed a sign near the ninth green. "To Help Save the Earth, We Are Using Reclaimed Water." A few lights had begun to flicker on in the condos adjacent to the nature preserve and I heard the buzz of a stone saw from inside one of the new homes-in-progress. My watch read six o'clock. In fifteen minutes, Laura would begin to worry. I sprinted for several minutes until I reached the wooden bridge leading through the marsh to the thirteenth tee. Although the early morning sky had begun to lighten from black to an eggplant purple, a thick overhang of swamp maples reduced visibility in the marsh. I thought I recognized the haunting call of a pair of sandhill cranes. Maybe the same fellows we'd chased off the tee yester-day. Then, over the clip-clopping of my Nikes, I heard a loud rustling noise in front of me. Just ahead, an enor-mous alligator crawled across the walkway and plopped into the water. I couldn't help myself: I screamed.

"Shut up, Cassie," I said aloud. "You're scaring the hell out of the wildlife."

I continued to run the length of the boardwalk, now imagining the echo of a second set of footsteps. I looked behind me, but saw no one. I thought of Dr. Turner in-structing his companion to frighten me. No need for that—I could do it perfectly well for myself. I glanced over my shoulder a second and third time. It would have been easy enough to hide in the shadows of the vegetation, but not so easy to follow me on the walk—unless you didn't care whether you were seen or heard. Now every woodland sound resonated with the possibility of danger. Damn, I

"Is that a rhetorical question, *Deputy*?"

"This is a murder investigation, Miz Burdette. The question was quite serious."

"Then no, she was not a friend. Which is not to say that I wanted her dead or killed her, either one. She was a difficult woman. I'm sure you are finding many others who feel just the same way in the process of your investigation. Why did you tell me you were the sheriff, Deputy Pate?"

He stared at me, his eyes revealing nothing more than a cold reflection of my own. It had probably been a bad idea to confront him, to flaunt his embarrassing exposure the night before.

"If it were up to me . . ." He paused for dramatic effect. Though as far as I was concerned, the only effect the pause had was to underscore how powerless this little twerp had turned out to be. "If it were up to me, you would be under arrest, Miz Burdette. The circumstances of being the closest person to two freshly murdered bodies seem entirely too coincidental."

"Excuse me, but I thought you said one of Dr. Bencher's patients had confessed to killing him?"

"The guy turned out to be a wack job. Big surprise, eh? Finding a fruitcake in a shrink's office. So we're still looking." He stared me down for several seconds. "Good day." Then he swaggered off, leaving me in a now-too-familiar state of heightened panic. Tournament or not, I had to help find the real killer. Regardless of whether Pate occupied a ground-floor rung in his bureaucracy, he clearly intended to stir up trouble.

My surrogate parents waited back in the motel room. "I'm fine. I need to shower. Let's talk at breakfast," I said, sweeping past Laura and Joe and into the bathroom in my best imitation of adolescent disdain.

"But it doesn't rule them out," said Joe. "Stranger things have happened. Do you think she was raped?"

I shrugged. "I have no idea. Incest, rape, who knows? I guess we should include all of them, whether it really makes sense or not. We can eliminate possibilities as we go."

"I'll take Turner and both Atwaters," said Joe.

"I'll look into the Ruperts and try to talk with the folks at the Deikon headquarters," said Laura. "That leaves you Walter Moore and So Won Lee." Laura picked up her tray and headed for the trash can.

"Look, Kaitlin made the headline again," I said. I read from the front page of the *Herald-Tribune*. " 'Kaitlin Rupert, a participant in the LPGA Sectional Qualifying Tournament at the Plantation Golf and Country Club was discovered dead on the grounds yesterday evening. Cause of death appears to have been head trauma by blunt instrument, reportedly a golf club.' "

I folded the paper in quarters. "The club used to kill Kaitlin bothers me," I said. "It wasn't a casual choice. When you think about it, an iron has a sharper blade—it would make a much better weapon than a wood. So it had to be someone who knew what had happened on the course earlier. Someone connected with the tournament. Or someone who understood the meaning of the experimental driver."

"Or someone who knew enough about all that to throw the club into the pit and confuse the hell out of the scene," suggested Laura.

"It's pathetic, when you think about Kaitlin's quote in the paper yesterday," I said. "She said she played every shot as though it was her last. And they *were* her last golf shots. She just didn't know it."

"Time for you to play golf, young lady," said Joe. "We'll work on these problems later this afternoon."

Chapter 21

⚐ **The** LPGA commissioner was holding a press conference in front of a small group of reporters and spectators when we arrived at the golf course. "This has been shocking news, absolutely unthinkable. Kaitlin Rupert was part of our golf family." He removed his glasses and polished the left lens with the end of his tie. He set the glasses back on his nose. "We have made the decision to continue on with the tournament in spite of the tragedy. We hope you will all demonstrate your support to Kaitlin's family by attending the memorial service. The service will be held next to the practice green at approximately four o'clock this afternoon. Questions?" He pointed to a small, thin woman in the crowd who had raised her hand.

"Are the rest of us in danger?" she asked in a trembling, reedy voice.

"The police have assured me that if they had a specific, reliable reason to believe the community was at risk, they would so inform us. They assure me that maintaining our

"Oh, God," I muttered. My putter dropped to the ground with a muffled thunk. "I'm so sorry about Kaitlin. This must be so awful for you." I hugged Gary and touched his mother softly on her hand. Margaret Rupert began to cry—from the condition of her mascara, I could see this was not the first time she'd wept today. Tears crowded my own eyes. I needed to back off emotionally and narrow my perspective from sympathetic acquaintance to skeptical observer. "If there's anything I can do . . ."

"Thanks," said Coach Rupert. "Since Kaitlin can't be here, we'd love to see you play well today." He startled me by gathering me into an awkward, one-armed embrace. "I know this is none of my business," he said. "But don't be a stranger to your father. Life is too short." Whatever ugliness had passed between him and Kaitlin, the sharp pain in his voice was real. Though Gary wouldn't be carrying a bag on the golf course today, he had the far more difficult job of tending his family's grief.

Once they'd left the practice area, I tried to step away from the feelings that had washed over me and review what I thought I'd seen: three family members devastated by the death of someone they loved, the pain made sharper by the rift that had existed between them before she died. Hard to find the face of a murderer there.

I stopped by the bulletin board to check the pairings. I would be playing with cheery Jessica from Michigan, and a woman I did not know, Maria Renda. My 153 still anchored the rock-bottom position in the field. The powers-that-be had apparently decided not to admit another golfer in Kaitlin's place. So much for that potential suspect.

"Mike's hanging in there," said Joe when we met up on the path to the first tee. "He and his caddie aren't getting along too well, but it doesn't look like it hurt him to have me out of his way."

look she'd had two days ago in the lightning shelter. Her blond caddie, again dressed in his good-guy cavalry costume, trotted off behind her.

"Hope she pays that caddie better than you pay yours," said Laura. "Now go get 'em, girl!"

The sense of well-being I'd experienced earlier this morning had evaporated. My three-wood felt like a baseball bat, my arms like stuffed sausages—all fat and gristle and no muscle, certainly no sign of the muscle memory that should have carried me through this kind of panic. Choking, I believed they called it—no matter what sport you happened to be in the process of screwing up.

"Let it go," said Laura.

"Let it flow," urged Joe.

"Let it snow," I said, suddenly hysterical. What the hell? At this point, there was no place to move but up, up, up. I was a double murder suspect, the very worst golfer in the field, and an object of pity to even the second worst. DFL, the caddies on the Tour called it. Dead Fucking Last. Why not swing freely? My drive landed twenty yards behind Jessica's, with a flat lie and a clear shot to the green.

"That's a beauty," said Joe, beaming with relief.

"It's a sucker pin," said Laura, "right on top of the trap. Just go for the fat of the green."

Maria Renda located her ball lying dangerously close to the out-of-bounds line. She took a fast swipe at her second shot.

"See what I mean," said Laura as the ball dribbled into the bunker in front of the green. "She cut it too close." Maria screamed at her caddie in Spanish.

"I'd hate to hear the translation of that," said Jessica, covering her ears with her hands. The two of us hit our second shots safely on the green and two-putted for easy

"Excuse me, Dr. Lancaster, but Ms. Renda is distracted by your commentary," he said. "While there is no rule against speaking with spectators, we would appreciate it if you would take care not to inconvenience the other golfers."

"Of course," said Joe. "I'm sorry." He backed away from the green.

"Joe knows etiquette better than any professional golfer on the Tour," I said to Laura once the official drove off. "Her game would be in the toilet even if Bob Rotella and David Leadbetter were both standing by to patch her up. What a pain in the butt." We marched on in silence: I was just mad enough to birdie three and four, and eke out ugly pars on the next three holes. Jessica played steady, unremarkable golf, and Maria Renda dug her own trench deeper and deeper.

"Somebody has a sense of humor here," said Laura, pointing to a hand-carved sign in the garden by the eighth tee: "Time to Stop and Smell the Roses." Nice sentiment, but not likely today. Besides, it was hard to smell anything other than the bleach used by workers powerwashing the windows on the adjacent pink condos.

After both Jessica and I had planted our drives in the fairway, Maria stepped onto the tee. She pantomimed her swing twice in slow motion. From the particular attention she paid to the position of her elbow, I gathered she was trying to correct her string of snap hooks. After shifting her feet to point slightly right, she blistered her longest drive of the day. Straight down the middle. No duck hook there—not even a gentle draw. However, with the combination of the adjustment in her setup and the fact that the fairway took a dogleg to the left, her ball headed toward a finger of the same pond she'd encountered on the third hole. It skipped through the rough and hopped into the water. Maria stalked off the tee and slammed her

By the time Laura and Joe rejoined us on the tenth tee, I had carded another birdie on eight and was flying high.

"I just missed the lag putt on nine or we'd be three under," I said. "Let me see the damage." Laura removed the ice pack from her temple to show me the thin slit of her swollen and discolored left eye. "Whoa, baby. That's a doozy."

The remainder of the round flew by without incident. A simple par on ten, a splendid birdie on eleven involving a seven-wood out of the fairway bunker and a long downhill putt from the back of the green. On the par-three fifteenth, I took a free drop away from mole cricket damage on my short drive and chipped in for bird from the improved lie. Maria's face told it all—a hearty disapproval for my taking full advantage of the local rule. Or was it anger at her own miserable display of putting? Whatever the facts of her inner turmoil, the fight appeared to have drained out of her after her tantrum on the eighth tee.

A small crowd gathered as we approached the eighteenth green. I remembered the scene I'd pantomimed in the moonlight before the tournament started. I executed a close approximation of the drive and approach shot I'd imagined, and just missed the long birdie putt. The spectators who waited under the shade of the live oak clapped enthusiastically as we walked off the green.

"A sixty-eight, you animal! You shot a sixty-eight!" yelled Laura. She picked me up and whirled me around until I begged to be released. I couldn't stop smiling. The sixty-eight, which threatened my best score ever in competition, meant an express ride away from the rock-bottom position where I'd started the morning.

He laughed, then cleared his throat solemnly. It appeared that he, too, was enjoying his short burst of fame. "In fact, however, this club had not yet been released, or should I say, unleashed, on the public." Another grin broke through, then he recomposed his serious expression. "We regret that our marketing representative did not follow company policy when he allowed the piece of equipment to be utilized ahead of its scheduled release date. He has been relieved from employment with our company." Poor Walter. The golf gods were really piling it on.

"Are you aware that the club was used to murder a golfer yesterday?"

Definitely a marketing nightmare.

The Deikon representative frowned. "We deeply regret Ms. Rupert's death and extend our sincere sympathy to her family. Otherwise, I have no further comment." He ducked under the ropes and stalked away from the press tent. The reporters turned to me.

"How was it out there today?" asked the reporter from the *Herald-Tribune*. Kind of a dumb question, but almost an obligatory opening for most golf interviews, and one I was delighted to answer.

"After the first few holes, I started to have fun, even though I left a few birdie opportunities on the course. But overall, my swing felt good, like I was hitting the sweet spot. Wow, what a time for that to happen!" Who was this talking? The reporters laughed with me.

"Maria Renda had a rough day. How did that affect your round?" asked the reporter.

"Yeah, she struggled." I searched for something non-confrontational to say. Truth was, on top of nearly sending my best friend to the great golf course in the sky with her temper tantrum, she'd been a royal pain in the ass. And here was my chance to let her have it. On the other hand, the women's golf world was a small community, and I

Gary's mouth reflected the sadness of the moment, sadness that would linger in the weeks, months, and years to come.

"A beautiful young life was taken from us yesterday, prompting us to remember that we do not always understand the mysterious ways of God. Jesus was no stranger to grief. He told us: 'In my Father's house are many mansions; if it were not so, I would have told you. I go to prepare a place for you.' " An edgy, lonely feeling filtered through me as I listened to the preacher's words.

"I'm going to look around a bit," I whispered to Laura. "I see Jeanine on the other side—I want to say hello. I'll meet you later at the car."

I needed to move around, and not just to scan the crowd for murder suspects or chat with Jeanine. A lapsed Presbyterian, I was just no good with death. I wished I had the unquestioning beliefs of my Catholic friends from childhood: go to church, take Communion, confess your sins, and presto, you had a place reserved in heaven. That kind of blueprint could take the sting out of dying. But much as I wanted to believe it, I didn't. I couldn't get the picture of Kaitlin lying cold and lifeless on the ground out of my mind. Or worse yet, incinerated to a handful of ashes and stashed in some hideous, but pricey piece of pottery. Maybe you'd expect it when someone old died— that was the natural order of things. But with a person like Kaitlin, so young and full of expectations for her life . . . well, even if she'd been annoying as hell while still alive, her death cast a shadow that blurred all the edges of what I could understand.

A representative from the administrative office of the Futures Tour introduced herself to the crowd. "We did not have Kaitlin with us long," she said. "Yet she left behind many strong memories of her short career."

around seven at the Starlight?" I gave her a quick hug and headed back to the car, where I'd planned to catch up with Laura.

"I need a nap," she said. "I've got a big goose egg and a headache to match."

"Can you find a ride home? I wanted to try to catch Tom Reilly, the publicity guy, before he leaves. Ask him a few questions about So Won Lee."

I snaked my way through the cars in the parking lot toward the LPGA office. In the row closest to the clubhouse, I saw the Deikon honcho unlocking the door to his SUV. "Excuse me," I called and trotted over to his vehicle. "I'm Cassie Burdette, one of the golfers. I've been very impressed with your equipment this week."

The Deikon man smiled and shook my hand. "We're always pleased to find a new customer. Did you have a good day today?" He perked up when I told him about my sixty-eight.

"I'm going to need woods and irons," I said. The rep's face crinkled into an even wider smile. "Who should I contact about trying some clubs? I take it Walter Moore's on the way out."

"He's out, not just on the way out. I'll give you my card, you can call me at headquarters," he said.

"How long did Walter work for you? It must have been a shock when all this happened."

"A couple years," answered the rep, his smile gone now. "I warned my boss not to hire him."

"You predicted trouble?"

"It didn't take a brain surgeon," said the rep. "A guy comes to you with work experience as a bouncer and a used car salesman, plus a manslaughter charge in his curriculum vitae. You be the judge."

"A manslaughter charge?"

"I'm ready for you, Cassie," said Tom Reilly, poking his head out into the hallway. "How can I help? I hope you're not here to complain about your write-up—it's already been e-mailed to headquarters and posted on the website."

"I'm sure it's fine," I told him. "I'm just curious about So Won Lee."

"That was a darned shame," said Tom. "From what I saw, she was a nice girl, and a nice player."

"I know you can't show me her profile," I said. "But could you look it over and tell me if you see anything unusual, anything that might possibly connect her to Kaitlin's murder?"

He brought out a thick notebook containing the profiles from the entire Q-school field. Mine would be there, too. Husband, no. Children, none. Hobbies, none I cared to make public. Organic gardening made me sound like a dork, and I didn't want someone goading me to perform hot licks on a banjo I hadn't touched in years. Lowest score ever, sixty-five, Palm Lakes Golf Course, Myrtle Beach, South Carolina. Lowest score in competition, sixty-eight, Seminole Golf Course, Tallahassee, Florida—a flat, wide-open layout that took some of the bragging rights out of the number. If I had planned on playing here next year, I'd be able to replace that score with today's round. Teachers or individuals having influenced your career—this blank was remarkable only for the absence of my father's name.

Tom interrupted my thoughts to read from So Won's page in the notebook. "She was born and raised in Korea, has been playing on the Futures Tour this year, enjoys time with her family, shot a sixty-two at her home course in Seoul, sixty-three this year at the Lincoln Futures Golf Classic in Avon, Connecticut. I don't really know what you're looking for, there's no question asking whether

vances down? This theory would raise Julie to the status of murder suspect, as well as explain Gary's dislike for her.

I found Jung Hyun Ro at the Panther putting green. She nodded politely at my greeting, then refocused on her putting stroke. "How is So Won Lee holding up?" I asked, dropping three balls down onto the short grass. "It was such a shame, what happened to her."

"She was very sad," said the girl. She sunk two three-footers. "It was not her golf club that they found in her bag." Clunk, clunk, two more balls deposited in the heart of the cup. "But she is at peace, if it is God's will. And she has forgiven those who have wronged her." I looked carefully to see whether Jung Hyun Ro was including me, the obvious beneficiary of So Won's misfortune, in that company. Her face was blank. I rolled a putt well past my targeted hole.

"Is she still in town?"

"She left for Orlando yesterday afternoon."

So much for the theory of So Won Lee as killer. It's hard to have a murder pinned on you if you were miles away from the immediate vicinity.

I returned my putter to the trunk, slid into the driver's seat of the car, and pointed it to the Starlight—home away from home. None of my ruminations fit just right. Walter Moore, with a manslaughter charge in his history, was developing as a solid suspect. Other than that, my latest brainstorm about Julie Atwater made as much sense as any of the other theories we were working with. Not a lick.

"Let's see, I've lost two contracts, a girlfriend, and my professional credibility. Plus, the cops are on me like flies on a cow's ass. Rough week? You make the call."

"What's next for you?" I asked after several silent moments. It was a clumsy question, but I couldn't think of a casual entrée into the subject of his plans.

"If I knew," he said, spittle forming little hills of bubbles in the corners of his mouth, "if I knew, I don't believe I would pass the information along to you. Some people are better than others about keeping quiet about subjects that are none of their fucking business." The last few words were more hissed than spoken.

"I didn't say anything—" He stood up and shut down my objections with a sharp wave.

"Well, good luck," I said to his back as he strode out of the room.

I flipped on the TV and surfed through reruns of Maury, Ricki Lake, and Queen Latifah. From this quick review, it appeared I could choose between programs about dictatorial husbands and fathers, gender-bending affairs, or two-timing gold-diggers. Who watched this garbage? And more to the point, where did they find the losers willing to expose their bizarre problems to public ridicule? I shut the television off—I was wound way too tight to sit through any of the available nonsense. The conversations with Walter's boss and Walter had turned the screws a little tighter still.

Returning to our room was not an option yet. Laura would kill me if I woke her up ahead of schedule to yak about my murder theories. That left pulling the trigger on the cocktail hour ahead of the others—not the smartest move just before the final round of Q-school. Or I could work some of my tension out in the miserable motel gym.

The desk clerk waved me over on the way through the faux green lobby to the small room that housed the ex-

wall. The bar targeted pecs with bungee cord counter-resistance and had a built-in spotting system that eliminated the need for a lifting partner. Who wouldn't want firmer pecs?

I squinted at the faint numbers on the upright sidebar. The weight on the EZ-Fit was set for forty pounds, which seemed ambitious but not unmanageable. As instructed, I lay on my back on the bench, with my chest centered under the barbell. I grabbed the bar with the overhand grip illustrated on the wall, disengaged it from its selectorized safety system, and lowered the weight to my chest. I braced my feet against the footholds at the end of the bench and slowly extended my arms to lift the barbell. It felt refreshingly heavy.

By the third repetition, the muscles in my arms and chest had begun to shake with the exertion; I was no longer feeling refreshed. Either I wasn't as strong as I liked to think, or the EZ-Fit could use a recalibrating tune-up. I needed to reduce the amount of weight on the barbell, or else quit. Quitting sounded good.

I extended my arms again and pushed the bar up and over into the safety slot. Instead of catching when I flipped the barbell over, the entire weight dropped and banged down toward my chest. By sheer reflex, I absorbed enough of the impact with my hands to avoid being knocked breathless or cracking a rib. I stared up: the selectorized safety spotting system had apparently failed, and the bungee cord cable supporting the weights had snapped in half.

"Stay calm," I told myself. "Breathe easy." Not so simple with forty pounds pressing on your windpipe. The scene on the television came into focus as I regrouped. Maury motioned the studio audience and the father for quiet.

collapsed, slamming my head against the floor. The barbell bounced off my windpipe and rolled up under my chin.

I lay stunned and choking, my eyes filling with tears. I fought back the urge to struggle against the weight across my neck. My left leg had caught under the bench as it fell. Each movement I made increased the pain. I wondered how long I had to lie here before another motel resident had the bright idea to work out. Certainly from the looks of the wall-to-wall, grime-gray carpet, the housekeeping staff did not often visit the gym.

From down near my hips came a familiar buzzing noise. The cell phone had dropped out of my pocket during the collapse of the bench and lay vibrating with the news of an incoming call. Although my hands were free, the phone was out of reach. The chatter of the vibrating phone stopped, then started up again. I shifted my body toward the phone, ignoring the sharp pain in my leg, and rolled over onto the talk button with my right buttock.

"Hello!" I screamed. "Hello!" I could barely make out the small, tinny voice on the other end.

"Cassie? Is that you? It's Mom."

"Mom!" I yelled down in the direction of the phone. "I need help!"

"I can't hear you. Turn down the radio. You'll damage your hearing with all that noise."

"Listen, Mom, please," I shouted. "I'm trapped in the gym under a piece of equipment. I need you to call the main desk and tell them to come and help me."

"This connection is terrible," said Mom. "It sounds like you're breaking up. Call me back when you get out of the dead zone."

"Mom!" I screamed. "Don't hang up!" Too late. The phone lay silently blinking. Even if she called again, I

The manager looked horrified. "We'll take care of it," he said. "We'll look into it. We don't need the police. We'll give you one night's stay free for your bother."

"You don't understand," Laura said. "Someone's threatened Cassie. This machine has been tampered with."

I crawled over to lean against the wall. "I think it was just a fluke," I said. Laura had already punched 911 into my cell phone and begun to explain the situation to the operator.

"I'm calling an ambulance, too," said the manager, apparently now committed to displaying his concern for my condition.

Several minutes later, the sheriff's deputy who had worked with Pate at the scene of Kaitlin's murder was shown into the exercise room by the desk clerk. "Not you again."

I smiled politely and explained my altercation with the Smith bar. The detective crouched down to examine the flattened bench.

"Why do you think this was done deliberately? This equipment looks like it could use some updating."

"Updating!" Laura snorted. "That's the term they use in real estate when the kitchen appliances were manufactured and installed in the Stone Age."

"All of our guests sign a statement when they check in," interrupted the manager. "The athletic equipment is provided for the convenience of our guests and all use is strictly at your own risk. Let's go somewhere more comfortable." He ushered us out of the gym and down the hallway into the breakfast area, away from the sight of the offending equipment.

"You're going to have to tell the detective about the closet," said Laura. "Tell him about Turner's threat." Joe and Jeanine arrived in the lobby as I finished reviewing

Chapter 24

Jeanine parked the car in the Chili's lot. She turned to assess her passengers: Joe in his blue sling, Laura with a bruised and swollen face, me with the thick, red, striated neck of a professional wrestler. Though the V-necked U.S. Open T-shirt I had chosen did not constrict or irritate my sensitive skin, it definitely failed to disguise the ugly swelling.

"All of you people look like you belong in an infirmary, not a restaurant," she commented.

"Nothing a few cocktails won't fix," I said. Once we were seated, with drink orders safely delivered to the waitress, Joe addressed Jeanine.

"How did you get involved with this person?" he asked, pointing to me.

"Oh, we met at Dr. Turner's office. Cassie was practicing putting while she waited to see him and we got to talking." She smiled in my direction. "She told me that her friend Mike Callahan would introduce me to Rick

miration of Jeanine suggested I hadn't been a hundred percent successful.

"Mike probably hit from the ladies' tees," said Laura. "Besides, he's been a professional golfer for over a year now; he's supposed to know how to play. You're just getting started."

"Look out, here comes Kaitlin's family," I said.

Joe jumped to his feet as the Ruperts reached our table. "Mr. and Mrs. Rupert, I'm Joe Lancaster. I'm so sorry about your loss."

Gary took Joe's offered hand first. "Gary Rupert. Thanks for the kind words."

I introduced Jeanine and Laura. Gary and his father accepted their condolences graciously. Margaret Rupert remained silent.

Then Gary noticed my neckline. "What the hell happened to you?"

"A little altercation with some exercise equipment." I explained the bench-pressing incident in the motel gym.

"I've never seen that happen," said Coach Rupert, frowning. He appeared relieved to move away from conversation about his daughter's death. "Sometimes my players disengage the counterbalance because it causes the weights to bind, but I've never seen the safety catch fail on one of those machines."

"Could it have been vandals?" asked Gary. His fingers grazed my neck. "Are you sure you're all right?"

"Fine." I smiled and did a little eyelash batting of my own. Mostly for Joe's benefit, I told myself—he'd asked for it. "I may not be able to talk a lot tomorrow, but in some circles that would be counted as an advantage."

"There's vandalism everywhere these days," said Jeanine. "People are just plain mean. They don't seem to think about how their actions will affect someone else. Like that club they put in the Korean girl's bag." She realized what

"Gross me out!" said Jeanine.

"Wow," I said. "That explains why he's so invested in this false memory organization."

"Turner's daughter's story is similar to that of Kaitlin Rupert and Julie Atwater," explained Joe. "Once she'd had several sessions with Bencher, she turned on her father, claiming to have remembered that he abused her sexually."

"Julie said Bencher never encouraged her, he just listened," I said.

"Whatever the truth, Turner was a senior lecturer in his college physics department at the time. The publicity finished his career there. Who wants a child molester on staff? First his application for tenure was denied, then they asked him to resign. He fought it for a year, but in the end, he quit and started the FMC."

"So he isn't a shrink at all," said Laura. "Cassie, you said he listed himself in the phone book as a therapeutic consultant."

Joe shook his head. "He has no mental health training of any kind. And he'd made life hell for Dr. Bencher up until the day he was shot. The FMC featured Bencher many times in their monthly newsletter column—'Dangerous Liaisons.' Each month several former patients would talk about their interactions with a so-called charlatan shrink. Bencher's name got to be a regular there. Somehow, they tracked down his list of patients and found the ones who were dissatisfied with his services."

"How did they find out who were his patients?" I asked. The idea of someone contacting me about my own therapist, or him about me, gave me the serious creeps.

"With the records kept by managed care companies these days, privacy is a lot less private than it used to be," said Joe.

in the closet. He might have gotten someone like Mr. Atwater to do the dirty work, but he sounds capable of anything, even murder."

Joe nodded and looked at me. "He also sounds paranoid enough to have someone follow you around and do something destructive to get you to quit snooping in his business. I'm not buying the accident-in-the-weight-room hypothesis."

"Turner would have had no idea I was going into that gym," I protested. "I had no idea I was going in there until five minutes before I went." I swallowed the last inch of my beer and motioned for the waitress. "I'm having one more," I told Laura before she could argue. "I deserve it."

"What about Walter Moore, then," said Laura, frowning. "Could he have known you were going to work out? You said you talked to him just before you went into the weight room."

"Why would he be mad at you?" asked Jeanine.

"We overheard a big shot from Deikon telling the press that Walter is history with their company," Laura explained.

"He has this idea that I was involved in exposing the experimental club," I said. "He knows I saw him showing it to Kaitlin back home, and I guess he thinks I ratted on him. Maybe he even thinks I teamed up with Kaitlin to put it in So Won's golf bag."

"Well, you are the one who benefited most clearly from her elimination out of the tournament," said Joe. "Believing that, the guy definitely had motive to hurt you, whether or not the thinking was twisted. He's lost everything. So he had nothing to lose. He could have set up the bench press accident. With the manslaughter charge in his background, I'd put my money on Walter."

"I'm wondering about the two different murder methods," interrupted Laura. "First, a guy gets killed with a bullet to the throat. In the throat, for God's sake. That seems really unprofessional. Then Kaitlin gets stripped, maybe molested, we don't know that for sure, and beaten to death with a million-dollar club. I don't see the connection. Maybe there isn't one."

Joe swallowed a mouthful of garlic mashed potatoes. "Try this one out. Supposing Turner had Mr. Atwater kill Bencher. Then later, when Kaitlin didn't bow out of the lawsuit against her father, he paid Atwater to rough Kaitlin up a little, just scare her away. But Atwater got overexcited and finished the job. If he molested his own daughter, I imagine he'd be capable of the same thing with a stranger."

"I'm feeling a little queasy," said Jeanine. "Do you think we could talk about something else while we eat?"

"Do you mind just one more question about the experimental golf club?" I asked. Jeanine nodded assent. "I'm not so sure Kaitlin really put that club in So Won's bag yesterday. Their bags look so much alike—maybe someone wanted Kaitlin eliminated from the tournament, not So Won Lee."

"Interesting," said Joe.

"Who do you have in mind?" asked Laura.

"That's the hard part, she'd made so many enemies. How to choose?"

"New subject," said Joe. "Are you planning to play tomorrow?"

"Of course! Why would you ask that?"

"Just wondered how you felt after the Smith bar thing."

"I'm already feeling better," I said, cramming the last bite of cheeseburger into my mouth. "After this and a couple Advil, I'll be good as new."

"Which baggage do you mean? Our father didn't travel light."

"Dad so badly wanted me to be successful in a way that he hadn't managed. It was too much pressure. I had to get away. Getting close to Coach was the only way I figured out how to do that. It wasn't subtle or kind to Dad, but I was only sixteen."

"That doesn't really answer the question."

"I know, I know. I'm getting there. Bottom line, Coach was really a lot like Dad. Hard on his players, expected nothing but the top performance we could produce. Underneath the crustiness, we knew he really cared."

"What about with his kids? His daughter? Dad pretty much gave up on me after you bailed out." I wished I'd been able to keep my voice from cracking.

"I'm sorry about that." He was silent for a moment. "I think it was different with Coach. He was disappointed that Gary wasn't much of an athlete, but really excited about what he saw in Kaitlin. I just can't imagine him hurting her. In any way, but especially that one."

"Lights out, for God's sake," Laura grumbled.

"I gotta go," I said. "Caddie Snow is giving me hell."

"Good luck tomorrow," said Charlie. "Be safe. And play well for you, not for Dad or anyone else."

I lay awake a long time, sad about our conversation. I missed Charlie. I missed my father, a fact that didn't too often surface through my anger. As I drifted off to sleep for the second time, I remembered that I had not called Detective Maloney. I'd put it on my list for tomorrow, after I finished the final round of the tournament.

Laura gave me a hug. "Then I'm with you. Let's go warm up the flat stick. Getting a couple of putts to drop today could be big."

"Ladies and gentlemen, this is the final round of the LPGA Qualifying School, the seven-forty-five starting time. On the tenth tee, from Myrtle Beach, South Carolina, Miss Cassandra Burdette!"

With the booming voice and the full-court-press introduction, I figured the starter must have had aspirations for announcing a bigger tournament than this one. The only fans available to respond to his broadcast were Joe, Jeanine, and the boyfriend of one of my playing partners. Their cheers produced a jolt of excitement that ran through my body, top to bottom. Smiling with encouragement, Laura fished the three-wood out of the bag and handed it to me. I rehearsed my preshot routine: sight the target, two quick practice swings, one final glance at the target. Then I nailed my drive down the middle of the fairway.

"You corked that one!" Laura yelled. I moved to the side of the tee for the other golfers in our group. Eve Darling hit a solid drive, as did Kelly Faison, our third playing partner. As we started down the fairway, I spotted Gary Rupert in animated conversation with Max Harding on the far side of the practice putting green. Thank God they weren't following us. I felt a backbreaking pressure already, even without a bigger gallery. Then I realized that I'd forgotten to add Max to the list of suspicious characters we drew up during dinner last night.

"What are you thinking about the approach shot?" Laura asked. I didn't admit I hadn't been thinking about the approach at all.

the tee. My head throbbed from the effort of trying not to think. I managed two average swings and two medium putts, and with relief, scribbled another four on the score-card.

"Do you have anything to eat in your bag?" asked Joe as he walked beside me to the twelfth tee.

"Didn't you get enough breakfast?"

"I want you to eat something," he said.

"I'm not hungry."

"Trust me, it'll keep you going," he said. "You have a lot of holes left to play."

I rustled through three pockets before surfacing with a partially fossilized Power Bar. Gnawing on the end of the bar, I watched the other two golfers tee off. No major challenge here—I'd made birdie and par the previous two rounds. A smooth five-iron would take me home.

But my mind kicked in with another agenda: a poise-sapping, fast-backward review of all the trouble I'd found anywhere during the first three days of golf. And then a quick, but also lethal, review of the trouble my playing partners had encountered. Any partners, anywhere. An ugly parade of shanks, hooks, worm-burners, rainmakers—all of which cost strokes, confidence, and tournament po-sition—flooded my brain. IMRAS. Inexperienced mind run amok syndrome. I'd seen Mike struggle with the same thing during his rookie season.

Swing through it, damn it, I told myself. Shut it out.

Too late. My muscles had already tensed in reaction and my tee shot plopped into the pond in front of the green.

I trudged toward the hazard where I would hit my next shot, remembering the only tournament that I'd caddied for Mike where he came in the money. We were in Crom-well, Connecticut, the final round of the Greater Hartford Open. We'd reached seventeen, the signature hole at River

natural and unexpected par. Stop the bleeding. Build momentum. Even before I hit the thing, I imagined it arcing up over the water, dropping down on the brown patch I'd picked out on the green, and rolling up next to the pin. And it happened that way—amazing.

I sunk that bogey putt, then eked out a bushel of pars and one lone birdie on the third hole. I'd long since lost track of where I stood in relation to the field. And Laura knew better than to bring it to my attention. There was no advantage to reminding me that the entire direction of my professional life rode on these last few holes.

As I stood on the eighth hole tee box, we heard voices raised from the direction of the clubhouse. I stopped in midbackswing. "What the hell's that all about?"

"Don't hit until you feel ready," said Joe. "I'll go take a look." He jogged off, returning to our group after I'd putted out.

"You won't believe it. They hauled Walter Moore away in handcuffs. It took three deputies to bring him down." Then Joe put his competitive, no-nonsense game face back on. "We'll find out more when we get in. Just put a smooth cut on this last drive. You're almost home."

Too tired to think about Walter's arrest or to try harder than was good for me, I hit the green three shots later, producing my second birdie opportunity of the day. I left the birdie putt short, but sank the par. A grin split my face as the ball clunked into the cup. After the other golfers putted out, Laura slung me over her shoulder and began what she called her signature Choctaw victory dance. "You were awesome!" she shouted as we whirled around.

"I left a few shots out there. . . ."

"Don't even start with that nonsense. We are finals-bound. LPGA Tour—look out!"

"Put me down, you'll throw your back out," I said. "Nothing's official yet. We have to wait for the other girls

groom. Maybe "Congratulations" for guys telling you about their weddings? Or was it "Best wishes"? Whatever. I certainly couldn't repeat the parade of expletives that had rushed into my mind.

"Congratulations," I said finally.

"Gosh, I'm relieved you're taking it so well. I was scared to death to call you. It sounds crazy, happening so fast and all. But when I met Masako last month, I just fell head over heels. She's really different from American girls. Not that you aren't the greatest," he added quickly.

"I'm no geisha." My only wish now was to wind this miserable conversation down fast.

"That's just it," he said. "She has a totally different idea of how the relationship between a man and a woman should be. It's like the women over here get what they need because they are serving the needs of the man."

And why wouldn't that appeal to him, a lovely Asian suck-up tending to his every whim.

"I know it's not feministically correct. It sounds crazy, but she explained it all to me."

"So she speaks English?" Obviously he struggled with the fine points.

"Some," he said. "She's learning."

She'd be learning a lot.

"Will she travel with you?" I felt a sick fascination with the details of his impulsive commitment.

"That's the beauty of the marriage deal," he said. "She doesn't work, so she can go with me anywhere and make sure I eat good stuff and get whatever else I need."

"Hmm," I said. Like get laid on a regular schedule.

"I'm so glad you understand. You're a doll, Cassie. I've been too embarrassed to tell you this was going on. I used to imagine us together—I even thought you could be my caddie. Who knows where it could have gone? But with

"Cassie," said Gary. "I almost fell over you. Congratulations! I'm so happy that you played well."

I smiled. "Thanks. There's only a couple threesomes left, so it looks like I'm definitely moving on up."

"Have you had lunch? Can I buy you a drink?"

"I'd love that, but I have plans with Laura and Joe. Can I get a rain check?"

"I'll call you when we're back in South Carolina. Great job!" He kissed me on the cheek.

On my way to meet Laura at the car, I dialed the Myrtle Beach Police Department. Detective Maloney picked up his own line. At the sound of his voice, I felt a rush of the rage I'd suppressed all week. "It's Cassie Burdette."

"How did it go?"

"Fine. It looks like I'm in. But I'll warn you, I'm pissed. That jerk you sicced on me this week not only made life miserable, he nearly ruined my shot at this tournament. He harassed me every chance he got. And he masqueraded as the sheriff when in fact he's a freaking peon."

"Slow down," said Detective Maloney. "Take it easy. Pate called me this morning and admitted you mistook him for the sheriff." He began to laugh hysterically, which did nothing for my mood.

"It's not funny. It's probably grounds for a lawsuit. And that idiot would not come off well in front of a jury."

"Easy, Cassie," he said. "I'm sorry. I don't think you'll be able to squeeze a lawsuit out of it—he just failed to correct your mistake." He began to laugh again.

"I can see this phone call was a waste of my time," I huffed.

Maloney's voice grew serious. "Sorry, but the idea of Arthur making sheriff is so unlikely. Now tell me how you played."

talked Jeanine into coming, too. Come on along and we'll buy you dinner at Sawgrass."

My gut erupted into queasiness. "Nah." There was no logical reason Laura shouldn't take the job with Mike. But I felt sick anyway. Dr. Baxter would have had a field day with the feelings that were making their ugly appearance. "I already booked a flight out early this evening. I'll watch for you guys on TV tomorrow."

"What are you rushing home for? Come with us."

"I'm exhausted," I said. "I need to just collapse. In my own bed."

"Any words of wisdom about carrying Mike's bag? I'm nervous. This is important stuff."

"Keep it simple," I said. "Use the old caddie maxim: Show up, keep up, shut up. The less you say, the less he can blame you for. Just don't take any crap from Mike. It's not good for him, and it won't help you either." This I knew well from my own excruciating experience.

"Don't worry. He'll think you're a pussycat when I finish with him." She hugged me. "Thanks."

I pulled away. "Thanks for carrying me through this week."

"You sure you'll be okay here alone? I feel bad about bugging out and leaving you here."

I didn't really feel okay about being left alone. But it was time to grow up and depend on myself, not lean on an entourage of old friends, supposed boyfriends, and headshrinkers. "Don't worry about it. You helped me get the job done. I'll be fine. I just talked to Maloney—he said they've arrested Walter Moore for Kaitlin's murder. They found his fingerprints on the Smith bar."

"No way. That's great. I feel better leaving you then." She turned and scanned the crowd, then waved to Joe. "I've gotta go. We're catching a cab to the Hertz office.

Chapter 26

Gary followed my directions to the little French place Laura had discovered the night she'd arrived in Sarasota.

"I have something to celebrate today, too," said Gary, after we'd been seated. "They nailed that bastard Walter Moore for Kaitlin's murder."

"That's great," I said. "Joe saw him get dragged off the course in handcuffs today." Gary's face looked sad. I fumbled around for the right words. "I don't mean it's great that they had to arrest anyone. It's not great that it happened."

"I know what you mean." He patted my hand. "I told her from the beginning that signing with him would cause trouble. Those clowns at Deikon thought they could pull her strings—tell her what tournaments to enter, what she could wear, you name it."

"Gosh, Kaitlin didn't strike me as the kind of girl who'd follow anyone's instructions, unless she saw something really big in it for her."

opinion, all the American Chardonnays spend too much time in the barrel."

"I'm sure it will be fine." Wine was wine, in my experience. "If it doesn't come with a screw top, I know it's special."

Gary laughed. He thought I was kidding.

"Where are your parents? How did they take the news about Walter? I feel so bad for them."

"I put them on a plane back home this morning," said Gary. "I doubt they've even heard yet. I'll call later this afternoon. If they're anything like me, first they'll be thrilled. Then they'll remember that Kaitlin's still stone cold dead, no matter who killed her or how many years he spends in jail."

"I'm sorry. What a mess."

"Anyway, let's move on to happier subjects. What happened to your lunch with Laura?"

I frowned. Not a happier subject. "Mike Callahan canned another caddie, so he talked her into pinch-hitting for the weekend at the PGA Championship."

"Wow, that's big time." The waiter arrived with the Robert Mondavi Coastal Chardonnay Gary had ordered and poured him a splash. "You swirl, then sniff for flavors," he explained. "The bouquet on this one is lemony and oaky." He motioned the waiter to fill my glass.

I sipped. "Much smoother than my usual Sebastiani from the jug."

"And it's not even in the same universe as Boone's Farm," he said with a smile.

I laughed. "Did you drink that poison, too?" I took another sip. "Delicious. I don't really get the bouquet thing, though. I guess my palate's not too sophisticated. I can tell the difference between red and white, though."

Gary chuckled. "You make me laugh, Cassie."

"So back to Kaitlin," I said, after the waiter had removed our dead soldier from the table.

"My parents always spoiled her. Whenever she had a problem, they bailed her out. She's the baby, they'd say. You have to love her. It was the same when I was growing up." I detected a note of bitterness in his voice. "Frankly, I don't think they did her any favors. She never felt responsible for her own problems."

"So when she was unhappy, she looked around for who to blame. This time it was Coach."

"I guess," said Gary. He drained his glass and pushed his half-eaten croque monsieur away. "Could we talk about something else? This is depressing."

"I'm sorry," I said. I arranged my silverware in an even row next to my empty plate. "So what's up next for you?"

"Find a job. Preferably not as a caddie. I'm not into heavy labor and I don't enjoy prima donnas." He laughed. "Though I'd carry your bag anytime."

He picked my hand up off the table and massaged the lifeline that ran down the center of my palm. Reflexively, I pulled my hand back. Too hot. Someday I'd figure out what I felt about this guy, but not today. Nothing felt clear in the confusing aftermath of the week's events. Old boyfriends, new boyfriends, no boyfriends. Missed the cut, made the cut, made the big cut. And dead bodies everywhere. I excused myself to go to the rest room. As I walked down the hallway, I noticed both a definite level of euphoria and a tendency toward lurching.

"Did you ever find out what happened with that barbell yesterday?" Gary asked when I returned.

"The cops think that was Walter, too." From the curious looks of the couple at the table next to us, I assumed the volume of my voice had veered too high. "If he killed Kaitlin," I whispered, "he'd already crossed the line once. He wouldn't have hesitated to do me in if he thought he

"If they hadn't arrested Walter, I would have placed my bet on your mother as the killer."

Although I definitely surprised myself by blurting out this unexamined and tipsy insight, Gary was speechless. "My mother? Where in the hell does that crazy idea come from?" he finally croaked.

"Maybe I spent too much time with Pate this week," I said. "But let's say she was mad at Kaitlin for accusing Coach of the abuse, and she tried to talk with her, but it didn't go well. Kaitlin refused to drop the suit. So then they got into a scrap and your mom hit her harder than she meant to." Gary opened his mouth in protest. I held my hand up to cut him off. "There's precedent for my theory—I saw them tussle on the Grandpappy driving range. Though Kaitlin definitely had the upper hand in that incident. Can't you picture it?"

"No, Cassie, I can't."

"Hey, do you suppose it's possible that someone else in your family molested Kaitlin? She seemed so sure it happened. I think I read a book like that once, where the girl thought her father abused her, but it was really her uncle." I laughed. "Maybe she even suspected you!" I warbled the music that introduced *The Twilight Zone:* "Doo, doo, doo, doo . . ." The couple at the next table stopped eating to stare at me again. "Hey! I bet that's what my dream was trying to tell me—that Bencher's lips were saying *Rupert, Rupert!*"

"I think you've had enough, young lady." Gary reached for my wineglass and drained the last inch of Chardonnay. "You're starting to hallucinate." He frowned and signaled for the waiter to bring the bill. It didn't take a genius to see that my teasing had gone too far.

"Sorry, sorry," I said. "Speaking of hallucinating, I saw you talking with Max Harding this morning on the golf course. You never did like him."

Chapter 27

I woke from a restless sleep, splayed out crossways on the motel bed. I was fully dressed, though wrinkled and sweaty, with a dry mouth and a heaving stomach. The alarm clock read four o'clock. The drapes were pulled shut and the room was dark. Was it afternoon or middle of the night? Damn. I had a bad feeling I'd missed my plane.

The details from my lunch with Gary began to take fuzzy shape in my mind. I was immediately grateful that he'd been gentleman enough to deposit me in the motel room and leave me here, alone. I remembered informing him that his mother would have made a logical murder suspect. How embarrassing was that? Next came the memory of teasing him about who actually perpetrated the abuse of Kaitlin. God help me. He had not been amused.

Someone pounded on my door. I stumbled across the room and peered through the peephole. Gary leaned against the door frame, looking fresh and cheerful, with

He began to massage my chest through my blouse.

"Please, Gary. Let's take it slow, get to know each other, spend time together back in Myrtle." At this point, I had no intention of spending any time with him, ever. But neither did I want to throw gasoline on the fire of his madness.

He rolled over and rested on one elbow, his other hand still clutching both of mine. He brushed a matted curl out of my eyes. "You couldn't leave things alone. Theories about my mother, analysis of Kaitlin's motives, you couldn't let it rest. My mother, a murderer?"

"I'm sorry," I said, now summoning my most earnest and reassuring inflection. "I had too much wine. I promise you I will never bring the subject up again."

"You and that fucking Harding." He leaned in and kissed me again, hard. Then he stroked my bruised neck with an unexpected tenderness. Both wrists ached from the tightness of his grip. "Why did he come to your room the other night?"

"He said he wanted to apologize for dumping me. I told him it was too late. That's it, really, that's all we said."

"Did he show you the photo?"

"What photo?" I was really confused.

"You're a lousy actress, but beautiful anyway. I regret to have to break this pretty neck," he said. "God, that sounds like dialogue from a bad movie." His laugh seemed almost normal. "What I mean is, if the Smith bar had finished you off, I would be spared the trouble. Though we'd have missed this fun."

"You set up the Smith bar to fall on me?" I was first furious, then very afraid.

"Of course not. It would have been a convenient, though unfortunate, end." I began to struggle to get away from him. Despite his pudgy, unathletic build, he was very strong. He rolled on top of me, pinning my hands

"Why did you kill her? You must have had a good reason."

He stopped rooting at my neck and stared at me. "After Kaitlin went to see Bencher, she thought she started to remember things about being molested by our father. I couldn't let it go on. Sooner or later, they would have blundered into the truth. I thought if I got rid of the shrink, the whole thing would fade away. But she was obsessed."

"So you did molest her."

He squeezed my wrists together harder. "It was harmless. Just kid stuff. But she made such a big deal out of it. She filed a goddamned lawsuit, for Christ's sake. I would have been ruined once she remembered it was me. My father would have seen to that." At the mention of his father, his voice dropped to an angry hiss. "I felt sorry, but there wasn't a choice. She forced it to happen. Same as you have. But we'll have some fun first, too." He began to kiss my face, then my neck and chest, all the while grinding his hips into my pelvis.

"Gary, stop!"

"What's the matter? I know you're no virgin. I saw you and Max on the beach that night. I even took pictures."

"You took pictures?" I was confused, then furious. Though under the circumstances, the news of this intrusion was hardly meaningful. "Why?"

He laid his head alongside mine and smiled. "I wanted you for a long time." He trailed his fingers between my thighs, then squeezed my crotch. "We would have been good together."

I squeezed my legs closed and struggled to push his hand away. "It wasn't going to happen, Gary. I was in love with Max."

"That's why I persuaded him to dump you."

I'd had a lot of theories about why Max quit calling me, most of them related to my shortcomings. Or his, with

"I wasn't," he said. "I wanted to show this to you before the police come. I wanted to finally explain." He pulled a Polaroid from his hip pocket and offered it to me. "This is why I stopped calling."

I accepted the photo. It was faded and creased, the white borders yellowed with age. The dark shadows of two figures barely materialized from what appeared to be sand dunes behind them.

"Hello, Max. This could be anyone. This could be anything."

He pointed to a white splotch in the center of the picture and cleared his throat. "I don't know how to be delicate about this. That's your bum."

I looked again. "It doesn't look like anything. No one would have known it was me and you."

Max looked sick. "I didn't know that. He said he had others. He said he would ruin your reputation permanently if I didn't back off. I believed him. I didn't know what else to do."

"Couldn't you have discussed it with me? Maybe I would have liked to have some input on being dumped."

"He told me not to. He threatened to hurt you. I'm sorry. Then it got to be too late. . . ."

"Not too late to come on to me the other night, right, Max?"

Two sheriffs' deputies burst into the motel lobby before Max could answer. Not that I would have allowed him another word.

"Gary Rupert's in my room," I said, scrambling to my feet. "*He* killed his sister, not Walter Moore. I knocked him out—nine-iron to the parietal lobe, if you want the technical terminology. I'd be careful, though, he might be coming around about now. And plenty pissed, I would imagine."

Deputy Pate, who'd skulked outside the interview during Max's questioning, broke into a wide grin. I scowled as hard as I could in his direction.

"When Gary came back a second time, I decided I had fooled around long enough. So I called these guys. And well, you know the rest."

"Where are you headed now?" asked Max once we'd been cleared to leave the sheriff's department.

I looked at my watch. "I missed my plane hours ago. I guess I'll just drive the rental car home. I can stop in Daytona on the way and look over the golf course where I'll be playing the second round of Q-school in October."

Never mind that useful reconnaissance of the golf course features would be impossible by the time I got there in the dark. Truth was, I needed friendly faces around me—not the kind that would hover over me saying, "I told you this was a bad idea"—like my mother. Or the kind who would hang around saying, "I really messed up, how can I make it up to you?"—like Max.

I called Joe's cell phone and left a message telling Laura to expect a roommate arriving after midnight.

putting green for a glimpse of their favorite players. Sheesh. This was a different world than the low-key buzz at the Plantation Golf and Country Club. Joe grabbed me from behind and folded me into one of his trademark bear hugs. All my plans to act standoffish washed directly down the drain.

"I owe you an apology," he said. "I didn't get a chance to congratulate you. I'm so proud of you." He hugged me again. "You must have thought I didn't give a hoot. We looked all over for you before we left, but you'd already gone to lunch with Gary."

I wasn't going to admit how bad I had felt about being left alone yesterday—lousy enough to have gotten trashed and practically thrown myself into a murderer's arms.

"I wanted to celebrate with someone. Maybe I jumped the gun a hair going off with Gary. It was not a good afternoon." I glanced over at Laura. "Jack Wolfe called just before you left to tell me he's gotten married."

"Who in God's name would marry him?"

"Easy, girl," I said. "This is my ex-boyfriend you're talking about." Laura lifted her eyebrows at that. "Anyway, her name is Masako and she doesn't speak much English."

"Which explains everything very nicely," said Laura.

"Time out, ladies," said Joe. "Tell us about Gary."

"We were having a pleasant enough lunch." I thought back over the sequence of yesterday's events. "He was a little snotty to the waiter, but other than that, things were fine. Right up until the moment I suggested his mother made a great murder suspect."

"You what?"

"I still think it was a good theory. We"—I gestured to the three of us—"never really talked about her, even though she looked suspicious all the way along. She belonged to Turner's wacko organization, she had a lot of

"I followed up with the sheriff's department this morning. Right now, Gary's not admitting anything," said Joe. "But his mother has been talking. Apparently she suspected that Gary was molesting Kaitlin years ago. She knew she should have done something. But Coach was always so hard on Gary; she thought he'd go crazy if she told him what she suspected. So she told herself boys will be boys."

"She knew about the abuse and she didn't do anything?" I said. "That's outrageous."

"But not unusual," said Joe. "People overlook the most incredible evidence in the name of protecting someone else in the family, or themselves, for that matter."

"I don't get it. Why would Mrs. Rupert have joined that kooky false memory outfit if she knew Kaitlin had really been molested?" Laura asked.

"She wanted to protect Gary, but she didn't want Kaitlin to get her father in trouble. She knew Coach hadn't done anything. I guess she hoped Kaitlin would just drop the charges, with enough opposition."

"She's got a forklift load of garbage on her conscience now," said Laura. "How's she going to live with herself?" She shook her head in disbelief. "I have to say, Gary Rupert surprised me. I really had my money on the phony Dr. Turner."

"If Turner didn't kill Bencher," I said, "why was he so intent on scaring me away from his office?"

"He'd mounted such a campaign of harassment against Bencher, he must have worried someone would take legal action against him," said Joe.

"Besides which," said Laura, "he made a darned good murder suspect. He was smart but sleazy and his tactics were just this side of guerilla warfare."

"Hit some short putts now," Joe called over to the golfer he'd been observing. "You want to start the round